SEMMELWEIS

Eclectics & Heteroclites 9

LOUIS-FERDINAND CÉLINE

SEMMELWEIS

Introduction by Philippe Sollers

Translated by John Harman

ATLAS PRESS, LONDON

Published by Atlas Press,
27 Old Gloucester St., London WC1N 3XX.
©Éditions Gallimard, 1952
Translation ©2008, John Harman
This edition ©2008, Atlas Press
All rights reserved.
Printed by Athenæum Press, Gateshead.
A CIP record for this book is available from
The British Library.
ISBN: 1 900565 47 1
ISBN-13: 978-1-900565-47-9

Contents

Birth of Céline

We always forget too quickly Céline's medical vocation. He believed in medicine ("that shit," he would say later, however), and kept it as a privileged way of seeing things, his writer's reason like his unreason endlessly pointing out the traces of where it could be found. Now this is the heart of the matter: there is a humanity that suffers and which dies for nothing. It should be cared for, should be healed, but in the end that is impossible since it hounds itself in its misfortune, and because the only Truth is Death. Therefore, the Devil must exist somewhere (otherwise, why does such a world of stupidity and suffering exist?). The physician is a social being, Céline is a social being, everyone believes that the only human reality is the social one; this is the realm of night, crossed by brief glimmers. Céline is fixed on that, as we know. It is he who gives capital letters to the words Truth and Death, just as we give one to the word Society. "Liberty or death": one day this was heard in French, a strange symmetry, a strange balance.

Dr. Destouches was thirty when he wrote his thesis on the Hungarian Ignaz Philipp Semmelweis. He already had some experience as a hygienist, he would perhaps become an authority in the field. But no: further than the butcher's is from war, from illness and from decomposing bodies, lies literature, that is to say a desperate attempt at understanding History as if it were pathology.

Pathology has no end, neither does History. Understanding it is already a lyrical and mystical engagement, a nervy illumination which insists that one be "intense, succinct and substantial". There is nothing falsely poetic in this attitude: vision should take part in a duel, should get its hands dirty, risk contamination and delirium. "Adapting his dream to all these promiscuities meant living in a world of discoveries, seeing into the night, perhaps forcing the world to enter his dream.*" We live, said Pascal, in a huge hospital for mad people. Has someone, in this tragic carnival, not lost their head? Will he be punished for it? Will he go mad in his turn for having made, on his own, a reasonable establishment of the facts which have escaped the blindness and the prejudices of his time? When Céline said:* "We must lie or we must die. I have never been able to kill myself", *one may believe that he is being sincere and logical. All the same, it shouldn't be impossible to say certain things when it comes to death.*

Consider this strange "Thesis" in its epic style. It begins like a clap of thunder (imagine the jury's faces): "Mirabeau howled so loudly that Versailles was frightened. Not since the Fall of the Roman Empire had such a tempest come crashing down upon men..." *We have here, right away, Céline's* clock: *the first centuries of our era, the French Revolution and especially the Terror, the war of mass extermination. What interests him here is fever,* "one vast kingdom of Frenzy". *His diagnosis is this: the thirst for blood, for cruelty, for carnage, is abruptly reversed, all of a sudden, into oblivion, deceptive peace, sentimental preachings, sentimentality. Who knows if a law for this couldn't be found here? Humanity would pass through phases of murderous mania to wash up, before starting all over again, on the beaches of nostalgia, melancholy and insipidity. At one moment charnel-houses, at others plaintive ballads. At one moment the egalitarian guillotine, at others the emptiness of the soul and chilly withdrawal. The assassins of yesterday, now become the moralists of today, swear by their great gods that never shall these horrors return. We know the tune, but it is difficult to shake off. It is like some enormous grinding mill provisioned with martyrs: Semmelweis is one such, and a big one at that. He was the one who put an end to the massacre through ignorance of women in childbirth in the hospitals of his day. Childbirth, Céline would say, is much more important than all the histories of sex. Here it is that one comes upon nature at work, that one can at last have a* "clear view of the straits ahead".

Semmelweis was an uncommon genius. He made an essential discovery, asepsis, but he sought to impose it in a clumsy manner. He had a flash of intuition, but he had a strong character and was rough with people. "Škoda knew how to handle men. Semmelweis wanted to shatter them. An impossibility." *In Vienna he set his sights on his superiors, especially Klein, an imbecile, but fairly, for the reason that he was* "the great ambassador of death", "for ever criminal and ridiculous in the eyes of posterity". *Daily reality meant routine, hypocrisy, omission (the worst of sins according to Céline the theologian), indifference, the pact in the shadows with death. Shall women not stop dying from puerperal fever? Pah, it's fate, misadventure, an expiation, the vengeance of God, perhaps. And besides, they're poor. Would all it take to save them, you say, be to wash one's hands after having dissected a corpse and then going off to manipulate a woman's uterine cervix? You don't say! That's absurd, you are making us tired. Leave off. It is impossible to emerge from what Céline called* "the obsession of surroundings". *No one had yet envisaged the existence of microbes, it would take rabies to set Pasteur on their trail (and Freud would still have a lot of things to say about Vienna). For the time being, nothing changed. The truth disturbed a secret alliance between society and the tomb. A crushing negative force was at work:* "But it is no less true that the span and the sorrows of men count for little, in the long run, compared to the passions, the absurd frenzies which make History dance to the score of Time."

Those lines date from 1924. People had emerged from hell, but a new storm was on the horizon. It wasn't by chance that Céline republished his thesis in 1936, at the same time as Mea culpa*. In between,* Journey to the End of the Night, "a Communist novel", *had led him to go and verify the proletarian paradise* in situ, *in Russia. A new hell. The consequence was fatal: as* *a writer "of the left" Céline became "an anarchist of the right" and the shocking pamphleteer of* Bagatelles pour une massacre. *In the image of his hero, he had just infected himself in passing. As Guido Ceronetti wrote:* "Céline is a formidable destroyer of stupidity, of futility, of stylistic emptiness, a furious avenger of the word, an authentic and veritable oracle. He has the dangerous usefulness of a Bible, but is an anti-Biblical athlete worthy of twisting and dying in the hated tentacles of his opponent. [...] With a Voltairean eye made darker through his own paranoia he saw it [the Bible] as an inhuman monstrosity, the germ of evil, the Semitic magnet of all possible wickednesses, a Sadean castle where the Hebrew Patriarchs piled up their massacres... [...] Who else has doubts about man, in the same way as Céline as much as in the Scriptures, feeling better about things, and when one wishes to flee the futile and the sordid one may put Céline's horn to one's lips just like the one in the Scriptures: neither of them yields."

Céline shows. *From the very first what is striking is his talent for drama. Here is the end of Semmelweis:* "Twenty times night fell in that room before death carried away the one who had issued it so specific and unforgettable a challenge. In the end, it claimed only the shadow of a man, a delirious, corrupted form, whose contours were being worn away by a creeping purulence. Moreover, what victory could Death expect in this most fallen place in the whole world? Who would quarrel over these phantoms of humanity, these dissembling strangers, these grim smiles prowling along the edge of the void, on the paths of the Asylum?"

Céline had good reasons for his intimate understanding of essential crisis, such as Semmelweis's, for example, sent mad by persecutions, and who burst into an anatomical theatre in the Vienna hospital, threw himself on a corpse with a scalpel, rummaged about in it and thereby cut himself fatally. Persecution? Infernal wickedness? But yes: "It even seems that infection might have been deliberately spread among the obstetrical patients for the ghastly satisfaction of proving him wrong." *Pregnancies, corpses: the short circuit, the least one might say here, was highly strung. There were, in this area, Céline insists,* "enormous biological powers in conflict". *Death, with a capital letter, would that be puerile? It's one way of seeing it. It would mask then the concept of nothingness whose form it takes, the generalised nihilism which gets built upon this error. This is why Céline was right, in opposition to all the well-thinking propaganda, to remind us of this* "longing for nothingness deeply established in man and especially in the mass of men, this sort of almost irresistible, single-minded lover's impatience for death". *A strange kind of love, one can see, and a kind it might be difficult to doubt could be more radically negative. Less human, in fact.*

Philippe Sollers
July 1999

Author's preface to the edition of 1936

This is the terrible story of Ignaz Philipp Semmelweis.

It might seem a little arid, or tiresome at first sight, with its particulars and figures, and detailed explanations, but the persevering reader will soon be rewarded. He will find it worth the trouble and the effort. I could have revised it from the beginning, refined it and made it more lively. That would have been easy, but I didn't want to. So I offer it to you as it is. (Thesis in Medicine at Paris, 1924.)

Its form is of no importance, the subject matter is what counts. It's as rich as could be hoped for, I suppose, and demonstrates the danger of wishing too much good upon one's fellow men. An old lesson that remains forever young.

Just suppose that today, in a similar way, some other innocent should happen to set about looking for a cure for cancer. He has no idea of the kind of music they'll have him dancing to! It would be truly phenomenal! Ah! let him be doubly careful! Ah! much better he be forewarned. He'll really need to watch his back! Ah! it would be far safer to enlist at once with the Foreign Legion! You get nothing for free in this base world. Everything has its price, the good, as much as the bad, must be paid for sooner or later. The good costs a lot more, of necessity.

At this moment when our profession appears to be suffering, with a fine sense of indulgence it must be added, a renewal of provocations on the part of a certain number of public sycophants, zealous hacks, born out of Romantic literature just as much as from the theatre, at the very moment when every layman, provided he has the free time and a few sheets of paper in front of him, claims to reveal all our faults and readily vouches for our blameworthy mentality, it is pleasant indeed to be able to dedicate this Doctoral thesis to the life and work of a great physician. We do not pretend to have chosen him at random, but nevertheless he was chosen and from a good many others equally deserving of appreciation. If I.P. Semmelweis is the one settled upon it is because medical thinking, so beautiful and so noble, and perhaps the only truly human thinking there is in this world, is exemplified most legibly in every page of his existence.

Doubtless any small amount of talent would be permitted to uncover other examples of such a force at work in the annals of medical destiny, less tragic if every bit as abundantly detailed, but the talent of the subject tempts our pen, and if we have become so much involved in the drama it is from a desire to be as intense, succinct and substantial as possible. May we ask for your forgiveness and understanding? We have not diluted the truth as regards any of the facts, even those most disturbing to the self-respect of our profession. Not one act of medical hostility, not one episode of inertia has been left out. Merciless towards all errors and follies, we have fulfilled this task in a spirit of openness, and far more thoroughly than any layman would have been capable of doing.

It is in this very way that we have wanted to prove to those easily influenced satirists who believed they had given us a thrashing, that talent cannot be a substitute for professional training and that those who are not doctors continue to launch their contemptible and trifling attacks while still believing that they have shredded the soul of our profession.

It has been said that appalling things occur in our laboratories; so many other things occur there that it would take a doctor to see and understand them.

Besides, are we obliged to defend ourselves? Let it be enough for us to ask of other professional sects that they produce examples of human beings as sincere, or as brilliant as I.P. Semmelweis.

As for replying point by point to those arguments which appear so utterly decisive to our detractors, such an idea should be discarded since we do not speak the same language. The world gets by only through the bounteous drunkenness of health, one of the magnificent strengths of youth, which is also characterised by ingratitude and insolence.

That too-sad hour comes to all of us, when Happiness, that absurd and superb faith in life, must give way to Truth in human hearts.

Amongst all our fellows, is it not our role to look this dread Truth in the face, in the most effective way we can, with the greatest wisdom? And it is perhaps precisely this calm intimacy with their biggest secret which the pride of men will find itself able to forgive least of all.

The Life and Works of

Ignaz Philipp Semmelweis

$(1818 - 1865)$[1]

---

1. Such was the title of Céline's thesis when it was first printed in 1924. The first public edition, in 1936, was called simply *Semmelweis*. The translation is based upon the former, which was cut and had certain details corrected for the edition of 1936. These factual corrections are incorporated here along with the punctuation changes made by the author to the later edition.

He indicated at his first attempt the preventative measures which should be taken against puerperal infection with such precision that modern antisepsis has had nothing to add to the rules he prescribed.

Professor Widal

Mirabeau[2] howled so loudly that Versailles was frightened. Not since the Fall of the Roman Empire had such a tempest come crashing down upon men, passions in terrifying waves reaching up to the sky itself. The power and rapture of twenty nations surged across Europe and eviscerated it. There was everywhere nothing but an eddying of beings and of things. Here, storms of interests, of humiliations and arrogance; over there, obscure, impenetrable conflicts; further off, sublime acts of heroism. All human possibilities — confused, unchained, furious, thirsting for the impossible — ran the roads and the marshes of the world. Death shrieked in the bleeding froth of her scattered legions; from the Nile to Stockholm, and from the Vendée to Russia, a hundred armies invoked at the same moment a hundred reasons for their savagery. With frontiers ravaged, melted down into one vast kingdom of Frenzy, men desiring progress and progress desiring men, here was the great wedding celebration.

2. Honoré Gabriel Riqueti, Comte de Mirabeau (1749 − 1791), writer, statesman and popular orator during the French Revolution. [Trans.]

19

Humanity was getting bored, it burned a few Gods, changed its costume and paid off History with a few new glories.

And then, the tempest assuaged, great hopes buried for a few more centuries, each of those furies sent as a "subject" to the Bastille came back a "citizen" and returned to its pettinesses, spying on its neighbours, watering its horse, satisfying its vices and virtues in that bag of pale skin the good Lord has given us.

In '93, they did away with the expense of having a King.

Appropriately, he was sacrificed in the Place de Grève[3]. When they sliced open his neck, a new sensation gushed forth: Equality.

Everybody wanted a share, it became all the rage. Homicide is an everyday function of the masses, but, in France at least, Regicide could pass for something new. They tried it. None dared say it, but the Beast was amongst us, at the feet of the Tribunals, in the bunting adorning the guillotine, its maw gaping. They had to keep it occupied.

The Beast wanted to know how many nobles the King was worth. They discovered that the Beast possessed genius.

And so the bidding in butchery ascended to formidable heights. First they killed in the name of Reason, for principles still to be defined. The best of them employed a lot of talent in uniting slaughter with justice. They succeeded badly. They didn't succeed at all. But what difference did it make in the end? The mob wanted destruction and that was all

---

3. *Grève*, in French a strike, as in "to go on strike".

that mattered. Just as a lover first caresses the flesh that has awakened his desires and believes he will remain true to his vows or a long while, but then, in spite of himself, hurries on... so Europe wished to drown in a horrible debauch the centuries which had raised her up. She wished it even faster than she imagined.

It is no more advisable to irritate the inflamed masses than starving lions. And so henceforth they dispensed with looking for excuses for the guillotine. Mechanically, a whole sect was designated, killed, and cut up like meat, soul included.

The flower of an epoch was chopped up into little pieces. That provided a moment's pleasure. It might even have sufficed, but a hundred passions that yawned with boredom at the slowness of such trifles upset the scaffold in one evening of disgust.

This time, twenty races threw themselves into a frightful delirium, twenty nations joined together, mixed, hostile, black or white, fair and dark, and rushed towards the conquest of an Ideal.

Jostled, slaughtered, sustained by slogans, driven by hunger, possessed by death, they invaded, pillaged, and conquered every day some useless kingdom that others would lose the day after. They could be seen passing under all the arches of the world, one after another, in one ridiculous, flamboyant round, bursting forth here, beaten there, deceived everywhere, sent back time after time from the Unknown to Nothingness, as content to die as to live.

In the course of those monstrous years when blood flowed, when life squirted out and dissolved in a thousand breasts at once, when backs were reaped and crushed by war, like grapes in a wine-press, a real man was needed.

With the first lightning flashes of that great storm, Napoleon seized Europe and, for good or bad, held it for fifteen years.

During the period of his genius, the fury of the masses seemed to fall into line, the tempest itself obeyed his orders.

Slowly, people began to regain their belief in good times, and in peace.

Then they longed for it, they loved it, they ended by adoring it, just as fifteen years earlier they had adored death. Quickly enough they began to weep over the unhappiness of turtle-doves, with tears just as real, just as sincere as the curses they had hurled, the day before, at the tumbrils of the condemned. They wanted only to know of sweetness and tenderness from now on. They proclaimed as sacred the devotion of married couples and the attentiveness of mothers, with as many declamations as had been needed to behead the Queen. The world wanted to forget. It did forget. And Napoleon, who persisted in living, was shut away on an island with a cancer.

The poets reorganised their timorous cohorts, a hundred sentimental verses were recited one spring day for the ecstasy of sensitive souls. They created with as much excess as they had once destroyed. A breath of tenderness caressed the numberless tombs. The necks of lambs never lacked for tinkling bells. Verses were murmured on the banks of every brook. It would take nothing more than a daisy in bloom to make a truly sentimental maiden dissolve in tears. And no more than that for a good man to fall in love for life.

It was around this period of convalescence, in one of the most colourful cities of the world, that Ignaz Philipp Semmelweis was born, the fourth son of a grocer, in Budapest on the Danube, in the shadow of the church of St. Stephen, in the height of summer, on exactly 18 July 1818.

In the shadow of the church of St. Stephen?... near the Danube... let's look for that house. It's not there any more today. Let's look again. In the world... In time. Something that may lead us towards the truth... Let's look! Far away perhaps in that round of frenzy which swept away... 1818... 1817... 1816... 1812... Let's turn back the march of Time... Of space now. Budapest... Pressburg... Vienna... 1812... 1807... 1806... 1805...: "On 2 December, at four o'clock in the morning, the action began in a fog that was not long in lifting..." AUSTERLITZ... That's not quite what we're after... we're looking for one of ours, our blood, our race, nearer to Semmelweis: Corvisart...! Corvisart...

He is not on the battlefield on that great morning of fire... Where is he? The Emperor's Doctor, his place is here!

Why did he remain behind in Vienna, at the General Hospital, where no orders could have held him?

Enormous building, that hospital! Sinister!... We shall return to it later, at length, with Semmelweis when his own hour shall have sounded. For the moment his destiny is not yet visible, or in the very place where his genius must shine: Nothing of him here.

The poverty of our senses!

In those wards, mixed with the civilian patients, soldiers from all armies lie prostrate everywhere, wounded, dying, surrendering their souls in any way they can.

And Corvisart... What is he doing at this moment?

Is he the celebrated doctor made glorious by association with his master's genius? Could it be through dissent that he absented himself that morning? Through jealousy...?

That is inconceivable. Medicine, after all, can only achieve a glory which is but slight. He knew that well, he who possessed all the scientific favour of his age, he who had been as highly decorated by his patient as anyone could be and who to his pride had been endowed with the highest professorial distinction: a chair in the College de France. And then, better still in those times of war: the Medical Service in the greatest Army in the world. Was he not, in such a fashion, just as envied, just as happy, just as decorated as any field-marshal?

Had he then some other desire, this ambitious doctor, apart from serving as a brilliant recruit in these sarabands of war?

Did he retain his own personal interests, welcoming progress in his art? In fact, yes.

During Austerlitz, during the most decisive hour of his times, he took himself away from his duties, without doubt tired to distraction, in order to translate, and with great difficulty what's more, an important book: *Auscultation*, by Auenbrugger.

Slow progress! Fifty years of silence had passed over this book!

Corvisart resuscitated it, gave it his own voice, and it became a very pure and very beautiful gesture in this man's career. Could he have better employed the formidable authority conferred upon him in his marvellous employment as doctor of the Epic?

Honour to Corvisart! A little honour too, perhaps, to Napoleon!

Thus through him we have ascended into the consoling harmony we were looking for, into that species of power which is so rare: compassion towards men. Let us return to Budapest, where our study leads us.

The soul of a man shall unfold there, with such great compassion, in so magnificent a blossoming, that the destiny of humanity will be forever softened by it.

L et us wait for them to appear, those days we are seeking in the womb of the Past.

First the dawn...

Truly, there is always the same feebleness, the same stupid stubbornness in the blind and deaf routine which surrounds the childhood of an exceptional being...

No one suspects... no one helps them... is the soul of the people therefore so far from everyday life?

In Budapest, it was the fourth son, Philipp, who was predestined... But his mother never suspected any more than the others. She was, they say, a hard-working woman, married young, rose early, pretty too, indefatigable, who was stricken down or good by a brutal illness in the winter of 1846.

Before that great sorrow there was much singing in the Semmelweis household, shouting too. Eight children!

The Grocery prospered, the little Semmelweises were well fed. Philipp was four years old one day, then ten. To everyone, everywhere, he seemed a happy lad; except in school. He did not like school, and this aversion was the despair of his father. Philipp loved to play in the street. Childen even more so than us have both a surface life and a deeper one. Their surface lives are very simple, a matter of a few rules of discipline, but the deeper life of the first child you may care to pick is the difficult harmony of a world that is in the process of being created. The child must incorporate in this world, day after day, all the sadness and all the beauty of the earth. Such is the huge labour of the inner life.

What can teachers do, with all their wisdom, to aid this spiritual gestation, this second birth, in which all is mystery? Almost nothing.

The being who grows in consciousness has as his supreme teacher Chance.

Chance is the street. The street changing and multiplying truths to infinity, simpler than books.

T he Street, amongst us?

What does one do in the street, more often than not? One dreams.

One dreams of things more or less precise, one lets oneself be carried away by one's ambitions, by one's grudges, by one's past. It is one of the most meditative places of our times, it is our modern sanctuary, the Street.

In Hungary, that country of melody, that country like a theatre set, peopled by a race more demonstrative than our own, music bursts out into the open air, effortlessly.

It was songs, and not school, that this little Semmelweis of ours adored. Temptation loomed large for him on all sides. In Buda in those days, especially around lunchtime, there were almost as many popular singers as there were porches in the street.

Why not pause here a moment?

Between the puddles left by the last rain, the singer, dressed in motley garb, comes to a standstill, scratches himself quite openly, watches the world go by... past his misery... He has a miserable little twinge of envy at all these people hurrying along to their midday meal... He, who yet has nothing, neither in his belly nor his pocket. From a piss-stained bag he pulls out a guitar with loose strings... The thing sobs beneath his dirty fingers...

He looks skywards, the wind...

With his sickly voice, he throws out a few searching notes; a few of us stop, and others with us... just as little Philipp did once. A circle forms and grows, crowding the pavement, getting in the way of passing carriages. A magic circle. This is it! Let's go. This wretch with his scratchy notes wants to lead us from our lives... and with what? With that... We'll see... Let's follow him... A little way into the Dream.

Noon passes, and this little group sings with a charm that hunger cannot quite dispel.

Their songs are neither gay nor sad, they are rich in magic or else quite lacking in it, those that have little are forgotten, but those that are rich go straight to the heart.

Just as surely as great music, these songs let us comprehend the Divine. Except that, with great music, one must be at least a little educated, a musician; to love the songs of the people, true songs, one needs only to love love, to have some feeling, and the words, they help too...

Listen with your soul, surprised and happy to be freed from a little of its shadow, to the charm of those four mingled notes... Four luminous notes, the gift of courage, the strength of hope that talent gives to those who know not how to... who are not joyful enough, believing enough, sincere enough, strong enough... to be happy.

But the music dies away... the circle breaks up... and the singer, slightly more tired, goes in quest of something to eat. Everybody is hungry. The gentle mystery fades... with regret in the hearts of all. The street falls back into being a gutter again. The tiny Church closes, the organs are stopped, it is sadder than it was before. There remain only those whom destiny marks for the eternal mass of infinite love. They form only a very small chapel of brightness, in space and in time.

But in contemplating the spiritual heights which rise on the other side of life, only vaguely perceived by the too precise scrutiny of men, have we not lost our way on the road of the everyday?

Nevertheless, events crowd in on us at every age, and should themselves bear witness, in their simple language, to the strength and the beauty with which every man prepares himself for the secret of his Destiny.

Those events arising in the first years of little Philipp's life teach us almost nothing.

At the high school in Pest where his father sent him, he learned the rules of Latin half-heartedly, without any great success either according to the prize-lists of the time. The classes, we know, were hard, Cicero difficult, youth uncomprehending.

Each Sunday, during those two years, Philipp walked across the noble bridge that spanned the Danube, going home for dinner with his parents, from whom he received so much unflagging encouragement and advice. The grocer was ambitious, might not Philipp want to become an auditing clerk for the army of Franz of Austria? Certainly, it was a very lucrative post, much sought after, filled by mounted arbiters who adjudicated on the disputes that arose endlessly between the troops in the field and the frustrated and discontented landowners.

But how far are the desires of a father from the destiny of his son!

For better or for worse, Philipp finished his first studies, and on 4 November 1837 he left Budapest for Vienna to go and obtain his degree in Austrian law.

This journey should take four days. An incident occurred on the outskirts of Pressburg that delayed the stagecoach. When he arrived in Vienna he was worn out and feeling sullen.

The first impression he had of the city was frankly unfavourable: "My dear friend," he wrote to Markusovszky, the day after his arrival, "how I miss our city, our gardens, our promenades! Nothing pleases me here..."

He never came to love Vienna. The real reasons for this antipathy were hidden, but life would later formulate them for him with the utmost precision.

Meanwhile, during his first sojourn in Vienna, he felt himself a foreigner, predestined to displease. All his feelings remained Hungarian, unfathomable. For a long time, he clung to this absolute faith in his own people, until the day when even his compatriots turned against him. There can be no doubt that it was decreed that he should be unhappy among his fellow men, no doubt that for beings of his stature all simply human sentiments should prove a weakness. Those who must create things worthy of admiration do not ask one or two private affections for the affective powers that will kindle their great destinies. Mystic ties join them to everything that exists, everything that pulsates, ties that hold them and often chain them with a sacred enthusiasm. They can never, unlike most of us, come to consider a beloved wife or child as the most vivid aspect of their *raison d'être.*

In fact, Semmelweis drew his existence from sources too deep to be properly understood by other men. He was one of those people — all too rare — who can love life at its simplest and most beautiful: life itself. He loved it more than reason.

In the Story of time, life is nothing but a delirium, the Truth is Death.

As for medicine, in this Universe, it is nothing but a sentiment, a regret, a compassion more active than others, and virtually ineffective in those days when Semmelweis was coming to grips with it. He entered medicine quite naturally. Law did not hold him for long.

One day, without notifying his father of his decision, he enrolled on a course at the hospital, then attended an autopsy in a cellar, where science interrogates a corpse at knifepoint... Afterwards, with others, standing in a circle around the bed of a patient, he had the opportunity of listening to Škoda, the great physician of the day, pronouncing on the condition and the future of a fever victim. Škoda was brilliant, he had a wealth of knowledge, great acuity, and characterised an illness as one might describe the face of an old acquaintance. During the night, the fever rose, the spirit of the patient escaped... Next morning, a rigid body, the fever vanished, the sheet drawn up... presently carried away. Autopsy... Škoda's erudition was again brilliant, his shrewdness sharp. They grew used to this, lost sight of death, saw only Škoda from now on, listened to him alone, one must die one day when one's turn comes, without too much protest... This is the price that must be paid for doctors' continuing fortune.

We must speak here of this Škoda, at least of his medical activities, for it was his influence which played the greatest role in the life of Semmelweis. He was, moreover, a man of the very first rank, enjoying a tremendous renown, which he had well earned. His clinical teaching was attended by an ever greater number of pupils, he could count on the active sympathy of the entire younger element in Viennese medicine. His practice in Auscultation, following the work of Auenbrugger, had been carried out with great audacity and provoked a storm of opposition. Because of this, his celebrity was marked by a certain heated controversy usually lacking in the solemn careers of scientists.

We might be permitted to take for granted the enthusiasm which led Semmelweis into medicine, but, in actual fact, we only know that very swiftly he became the close pupil of Škoda and that the Faculty of Law registered his failure before he had even been awarded his first diplomas.

Of his father's opinion on hearing the news of this sudden transfer we know nothing.

Through Škoda's teaching, Semmelweis learned what the clinical mind was capable of in probing nature, and if, in this domain, he never acquired the subtlety of his master, his achievements were more solid, for he was to probe much further into Truth.

Another man, less renowned than Škoda, especially less outspoken than he, but whose work possessed a much greater importance, enriched Semmelweis's thought with an indispensable scientific method. This master was Rokitansky.

Rokitansky occupied the first chair of pathological anatomy in the Faculty of Vienna. It was there that he laid the foundations of that great school of histopathological research in Central Europe whose works were so numerous and memorable. Semmelweis was one of his admirers from the beginning; what he then learned seems always to have been a part of his most useful and most urgent preoccupations.

We may ask by what action and what providential harmony the disasters of puerperal fever, until then hermetically sealed from investigation and altogether horrifying, might be obliterated by the modest discipline instilled in the mind of his pupil by Rokitansky? The audacities of progress are fragile! We tremble, in fact, as we think of the perils through which it was steered, still more the futilities of which it was relieved during its triumphal march. Genius has no small resources, only the possible or the impossible exist. At that time, in the entire field of microscopy, no truth had travelled very far along the road to the Infinite, the powers of the boldest, the most scrupulous researcher stopped short at Pathological Anatomy.

Beyond these few highly-coloured embellishments, along the path of understanding infection, there was nothing but death and words...

Such were the essential tools Semmelweis received from his two teachers. But these were not all they gave him. Over the years, they followed with anxious eyes the labours and the advances of their unforgettable disciple. With a great deal of sadness they watched him mounting the steps of his calvary, and could not always understand him.

Seeking to support him, to counsel him, they often tried to check his impetuous outbursts, tried to convince him of the futility of his insolence, of his interminable polemics with dishonest adversaries. During those years of his pitiless ordeals, when the pack of enemies howled its hatred of the Semmelweis it had tracked down and banished, these two masters, grown old and tired nonetheless of personal combats, united once more to defend him. Škoda knew how to handle men. Semmelweis wanted to shatter them. An impossibility. He wanted to thrust himself through every stubborn door, he injured himself cruelly. Those doors would not open until after his death.

We owe it to the truth to set down the one great fault Semmelweis had: his savagery in all things, and especially towards himself.

In Vienna, already, after knowing him for only a few months, Škoda had to intervene to prevent his pupil from drifting into a great moral anguish, as the result of exhaustion.

Quick-tempered and hypersensitive to the trivial jokes the other students indulged in at the expense of his pronounced Hungarian accent, he came to believe himself the victim of persecution. He was on the verge of an obsession. Škoda calmed the young man down, gently made him admit his mental exhaustion, and insisted that he take a long period of rest. This advice was soon supported by letters from his alarmed mother. At last this all decided Semmelweis to take a long and necessary holiday.

In the spring of 1839, he set out once more for Budapest, where he was impatiently awaited. The joys of home-coming, the rediscovered warmth of home, long walks through the bustling streets, such distractions restored his temperament, strengthened his health, but could not placate his spirit. He grew bored.

However, the new School of Medicine in Budapest had just opened its doors. He registered there. But the teaching there did not satisfy him. He said so; his remarks were repeated. Rumours followed him. In

1841, he turned once more towards his masters in Vienna. There was no shift in their attitude towards him; but he, in contrast, had undergone a profound change. That became evident when Rokitansky sought to persuade Semmelweis to undertake some lengthy research work on the vicissitudes of hepatic tissue, or when Škoda sought to make him concentrate upon the stethoscopic technicalities for which he had shown some talent. He refused point-blank. And their surprise then became so painful to him that he avoided their amphitheatres for a time and even ceased for a period of several months to visit the hospitals.

It seemed to him then that the activities of the Medical Faculty were too subtle, too theoretical, too useless in a word, from the point of view of the patients to whom his own thoughts were increasingly turning.

During the period of this vocational crisis, Semmelweis would prefer long walks in the botanical gardens, where he consulted a plant expert named Bozatov, inexhaustible in his knowledge of the virtues of simples. The wholly empirical science of this herbalist delighted Semmelweis. Captivated by this theme, he began to read the interminable histories of this subject. In their music of healing, even though vague and not free from quackery, he discovered a flawless charm. For months he gave himself over to this simple therapy; he no longer had any enthusiasm for Škoda's certitudes, or for Rokitansky's hair-splitting. And when the time came to decide upon a subject for his thesis, we find him still completely saturated with such feelings.

It surprises him.

The work would be short: barely twelve pages.

But twelve pages of dense poesy, and rustic imagery. In accordance with the Classical tradition then in vogue, it was written in Latin, but in the simplest Latin possible. It was entitled *On the Life of Plants*. It served as an excuse to celebrate the characteristics of the rhododendron, the Easter daisy, the peony and several other plants.

Incidentally, the author is pleased to inform us of phenomena of prime importance, yet usually taken for granted, among other things that if the heat of the sun is favourable to the blooming of flowers, cold on the contrary is entirely harmful to them.

There could be nothing simpler, yet there is pathos in the following:

"What spectacle," he wrote, "can rejoice the heart and mind of a man more than plants! Than these glorious flowers with their marvellous variety, exhaling their delicate odours! Which furnish to our taste the most delicious saps! Which nourish our bodies and heal it of its maladies! The spirit of plants has inspired the cohort of poets of the divine Apollo, who marvelled already at their countless forms. Man's reason cannot bring itself to understand such phenomena on which it can shed no light but which natural philosophy adopts and respects. From all that lives, in fact, emanates the omnipotence of the Divine."

This thesis contains many other passages of the same harmonious inspiration and of equal value.

His master Škoda, who presided over the Faculty jury, asked Semmelweis, doubtless so as not to be left out of the discussion, whether it might be possible to replace mercury with the sap of certain flowers in the treatment of illnesses, and asked him to defend the delicate subject of "Medicine and Sentiment". The whole thing in bad Latin, it goes without saying.

The essential point for us to know is that he was received as a doctor of medicine on that day, a date some authors place in March and others in May, in any event during the spring of 1844.

As we know, Škoda was not only a remarkable clinician, but his intuitive shrewdness and sagacity, amply displayed in his scientific works, also served him greatly in the course of his brilliant career.

Having associated with Semmelweis for some five consecutive years, there can be no doubt that he held then a very clear opinion of his pupil. Certainly Škoda sensed in this young Hungarian all those powers of discovery with which he was familiar in himself, and of their value and general balance. We cannot conclude from this that at that moment he felt a touch of jealousy, but he took meticulous care of his own success and intended to remain the uncontested master of the internal clinic in Vienna.

Now, while his own recently-published *Treatise on Auscultation* certainly contained incontestable discoveries, at the same time it included a great deal of subtle argument.

His opponents were not slow to make themselves heard, and, every day, Škoda was called upon to defend his scientific opinions, none of which seemed to be yet proven or accepted.

It was a difficult moment and Škoda knew, on the other hand, better than anyone, that pupils who are too brilliant are, as a rule, the most fearful destroyers of their Masters. Without doubt it was this presentiment that made him dread seeing Semmelweis, so eager and so ardent, catch up with those masterly teachings in internal medicine in which he exercised his own brilliant but fragile supremacy.

Once he had forgotten *On the Life of Plants*, Semmelweis naturally turned again to Škoda.

Škoda greeted him with a great deal of pleasure, and managed to foster in him the hope of an appointment in his own clinic. Specifically, he set aside for him, whilst waiting for something better, some small assistant-teaching at his side.

Semmelweis was grateful. But in September 1844, when the official competition for assistant to Škoda was opened and for which he put himself forward in the tests, full of confidence, a rival emerged: Dr. Löbl.

Semmelweis was defeated.

Škoda did not hesitate to invoke the inevitable question of age, which did in fact favour Löbl, to explain this setback.

"It is also a matter of patience," he said, "and since the next competition will soon be opened, everything should get sorted out!" A plausible enough excuse, it must be said, but it served his own interests so well that one cannot resist finding in it a suggestion of Škoda's scheming.

However, we must not go too far here in judging harshly his sincerity when it came to Semmelweis. Certainly, Škoda still liked him, but in line with certain rules of prudence and aloofness from which he did not care to depart. Was he perhaps right? One may love the warmth of the fire, but no one wishes to be burned by it. Semmelweis was the fire.

In short, we find him more or less consoled, waiting in Škoda's shadow for his own turn in the light. Doubtless he would have remained there for several years if Rokitansky, whose research at the time into Infection brought him into daily contact with surgery, had not directed Semmelweis, with his enthusiasm for healing, into this practice which was then nought but ignorance and disaster. It must be remembered, in fact, that before Pasteur more than nine operations out of ten, on average, ended in death or infection, which was only a slow and even crueller death.

We can understand that with such slight chances of success, operations were only very rarely undertaken. A small number of surgeons, almost superfluous even so, quarrelled over the three or four official posts in Vienna.

It was in their company that Semmelweis experienced his first disgust for those symphonies of verbiage which surrounded the whole problem of infection in all its complexities. They were almost endless.

It became a game of skill to explain death by "thickened pus", "benign pus" or "laudable pus". Basically, a fatalism in fancy words, the braying of the impotent.

Each of these surgeons, too pleased with having attained the high honours that were open to them, cared little for sincerity. Apart from Rokitansky, this group offered little hope for the future of men.

Semmelweis's naturalist's optimism, which ran through his Thesis, underwent a severe trial.

He would never forget it.

And it was towards the end of those two years spent in surgery that he wrote, with that vitriolic point which already characterised his impatient pen: "Everything they are trying to do here seems to me quite futile, deaths follow one another with regularity. They go on operating, however, without really seeking to find out why one patient succumbs rather than another in identical circumstances."

And in looking over these lines we can say that something has come to pass!

That his pantheism has been buried. That he is on the point of revolt, that he is on the road of light! Nothing henceforth will stop him again. He does not yet know in what manner he is going to undertake the far-reaching reform of this cursed surgery, but he is the man for this mission, he feels it, and the most striking thing is that in a short time it was to be achieved. As the result of a brilliant examination,

Semmelweis was appointed master of surgery on 26 November 1846. But, since there was no vacancy in any of the possible chairs, he became impatient. And the more so because the remittances he had been receiving from his family were becoming infrequent, and because his relatives were urging him to finish his studies and set up a practice, for they feared that soon it would be quite impossible for them to provide for his wants. His father had fallen ill; the grocery, doubtless because of this, had lost a measure of its prosperity. Semmelweis confided these troubles to his masters, who instantly used all their influence to report his case to the Minister.

Things began to move rapidly.

Since surgery offered no position, it was to lying-in that they turned. Klein needed an assistant, and was offered Semmelweis. But the latter didn't have the required diplomas. In the course of two months he passed all the necessary tests.

Accepted as Doctor of obstetrics on 10 January 1846, he was appointed assistant professor to Klein on 27 February of the same year. Henceforth he was to act as a member of the staff of the Vienna General Hospital, in which Professor Klein directed one of the obstetric clinics. Intellectually, this Klein was a poor individual, self-centred and strictly mediocre. All the authorities stress these characteristics at length. No one would have been surprised then at his display of ferocity when he sensed the first revelations of genius in his assistant. This was but the matter of a few months. Barely had he had the time to consider the truth about puerperal fever than he became determined to stifle this truth by all means, by every influence at his disposal.

He thereby made himself for ever criminal and ridiculous in the eyes of posterity, for in taking this attitude he revealed a miserable talent for deploying all his jealousies and all his stupidities against Semmelweis and against the blossoming of his discovery.

It was not only his innate stupidity which made him dangerous, but the fact that his authority was bolstered by the prestige he enjoyed at Court.

In this extraordinary drama which played out around puerperal fever, Klein was the great ambassador of death. "It will be to his eternal shame...," wrote Vernier later in speaking of his disastrous influence, of his peevish and imbecilic obstructions.

All of which, surely, reveals the great and beautiful aspect of justice. However, is there not another side which the impartial historian should be forbidden to ignore?

No matter how high, in fact, one may be lifted by genius, no matter how pure may be the truths one voices, have we the right to disregard the formidable power of simple absurdities? In the chaos of this world, consciousness is but a tiny light, precious but fragile. One cannot light a volcano with a candle. The earth cannot be knocked into the sky with a hammer.

For Semmelweis, as for how many other precursors, it must have been agonising to submit to the whims of stupidity, especially when he possessed a discovery so dazzling, so important to the good of humanity, as the one he demonstrated every day in Klein's obstetric clinic.

But in the end we cannot help thinking, even so, as we re-read the acts of this tragedy in which both Semmelweis and his work succumbed, that with a greater care for conventions, with a little more discretion in his demeanour, Klein, so puerile in his arrogance, could not have found the all-too-real basis for the complaints he uttered against his assistant.

Semmelweis dashed himself against obstacles which, there is little doubt, most of the rest of us would have overcome by the exercise of simple prudence, and elementary politeness. He lacked, or neglected, it seems, that indispensable respect for the futile conventions of his time, of all times in fact, without which stupidity becomes an uncontrollable force.

In human terms, he lacked tact.

T wo lying-in pavilions, identical in construction, adjacent to each other, stood in that year of 1846 in the middle of the gardens of the General Hospital in Vienna. Professor Klein was the director of one of them; the other had been under the supervision of Professor Bartsch for almost four years.

Through these gardens covered in snow, subjected to the hoar-frost of an implacable wind, Semmelweis made his way to take up his new position on the morning of 27 February.

He expected to find even greater sorrows in this new career than he had encountered hitherto in the surgical wards, but he could not have imagined what depths of emotion, what intense human tragedies were to unfurl on a daily basis in the wards of Professor Klein.

The very next day Semmelweis was caught, dragged and battered in that danse macabre which never let up in and around these two terrifying pavilions. It was a Tuesday. He was to register the admission of pregnant women from the more overcrowded parts of the city.

Only those in the utmost miserable state, evidently, would resign themselves to giving birth in a hospital with so woeful a reputation.

From their hesitant confidences, Semmelweis learned that while the risks from puerperal fever were great in the clinic Bartsch supervised, the mortality rates in Klein's wards at certain times meant almost certain death.

These had become accepted facts for the women of the city, and constituted from this moment the premises upon which Semmelweis would seek the truth.

Women "in labour" were admitted then to the two clinics on alternate days. That Tuesday, upon the stroke of four o'clock, the doors to Bartsch's clinic were closed, and those to Klein's were opened...

At Semmelweis's very feet, scenes so poignant, so affectingly tragic, were then enacted that upon reading accounts of them one is shocked, despite so much evidence to the contrary, not to feel an absolute enthusiasm for progress.

"One woman," he said later in speaking of that first day, "was stricken suddenly with labour pains in the street at about five o'clock in the afternoon... She had no home... she hastened to the hospital, but realised right away that she was too late... here was this woman pleading, begging to be admitted to Bartsch's clinic on her life and on behalf of her other children... she was refused this favour. She was not the only one!"

From that moment, the waiting-room became a pyre of blazing

desolation, where twenty families sobbed in supplication... frequently and forcibly dragging forward the woman or mother whom they had brought along.

Almost always they preferred to give birth in the street itself, where indeed the risks were far fewer.

Into Klein's wards, in short, went only those stricken suddenly, without a penny, without security, lacking even a supporting arm to warn them against the dangers of that terrible place. For the most part they were the most crushed creatures, the most outcast by the uncompromising morality of the time: they were almost all adolescent mothers.

In the context of Semmelweis's destiny, in which great sorrows seem nevertheless everyday, these griefs at times fell so heavily that they verged upon the absurd.

Hardly, in fact, had he made his first and saddening contact with his new functions, hardly had he managed to withdraw sufficiently so as not to hear the wailing of those the Hour condemns... than he received two letters, the first announcing the death of his mother, and the other the death of his father only a few days later.

In the account of this life, one seems to use up all expressions for unhappiness. The terminology upon which we must rely again and again to follow him in his work seems to derive almost entirely from the mournful tapestry of funerary pronouncements.

But the facts were even more sombre, if possible, than their description. That heavy sense of fatality which reigned in Klein's wards henceforth surrounded him. It crushed men, women, and everything else that was drawn into its sphere. He alone rejected this Destiny and was not crushed by it, but he suffered from it more than all the rest, in all those places where it stalked, in Vienna, just as much as in Paris, in London, as in Milan. Everywhere, sooner or later, had had to submit to the passage of the puerperal scourge. Hypocritically, in the indifferent shadows, they had signed a pact with Death. And if the wisest yet roused themselves from time to time with clever suppositions, that was because they had drained the petty resources of their own little talents, and when they never got anywhere they soon took refuge in official procedure. The fever of the childbearing! Vengeful Goddess! Hateful! but nothing out of the ordinary!

Perforce, this fever seemed to be just another of those cosmic and inevitable catastrophes...

The pious and despicable slaves of procedure looked upon this fever, without admitting as much, as a sort of sorrowful tribute commonly exacted from the women of the masses as an entrance fee into motherhood.

At times others, shielded from such professional habit, grew indignant, frantic, loud in their protestations...

It was then that Commissions were set up.

They were always made up of responsible medical authorities.

How easy it would be to ridicule all those successive, interminable Commissions! Let us try, however, to assess their efforts.

These were fruitless as ever during the fresh puerperal outbreak of 1842 in the Klein wards, when 27% of those lying in succumbed in August, 29% in October of the same year, and an average of 33 deaths per hundred was even reached in the month of December.

Over many years, plenty of other Commissions had admitted defeat in the face of this same problem. Among all those that had been appointed, one of the least inefficacious was perhaps that convoked by Louis XVI during the puerperal epidemic of 1774, which decimated the Hotel-Dieu in Paris. On that occasion, it was the milk which was blamed and as a measure against this epidemic the Paris College of Physicians proposed to the King the closing of all the maternity wards, and the isolation of wet-nurses.

Which was neither very wise nor very foolish.

In Vienna again, in the month of May 1846, an Imperial Commission was convened as an emergency measure, statistics this time announcing the mortality rates as ninety-six per cent in the Klein wards. What are we to think of all those who made up such Commissions? Were they as individually ignorant then, as inadequate as the measures they proposed? Not at all. But they were lacking in genius, and a great deal of that was needed in order to disentangle the skeins of disease before Pasteur had lent his light to the mediocre.

Besides, is not genius always needed in those crucial circumstances of this world, when the torrent of material and spiritual powers, obscure, confused, sweeps men along with it, in howling but docile crowds, towards bloodthirsty ends? Very few even of the most gifted know at such moments how to do anything except plot a more rapid course towards the abyss, or shout more loudly than the rest. Rarest of all is he who, finding himself at the centre of that obsession of circumstance we call Fate, dares, and finds in himself the courage that is needed to confront the common Destiny that drags him along. In the shadows he may find the key to mysteries that had before seemed insoluble. Almost always he who wishes for it with a great enough faith will discover it, for it has always existed; and the boldness of such a man is capable of diverting the torrent of fatalities towards other errors until the day a new genius appears.

Semmelweis chose this task in the awareness of his own capabilities and those of his time. Later, he himself came to recognise his role among men.

"Destiny chose me," he wrote, "to be a missionary of truth as to the means that must be taken to avoid and to combat the puerperal scourge. For a long time I have ceased to reply to the attacks that are constantly aimed at me; the order of events must prove to my adversaries that I was completely in the right, without the necessity of my indulging in polemics which can henceforth serve no purpose in advancing the truth."

In other areas we have become habituated to such declarations on the part of thinkers and politicians, solemn, but not based upon any precise or stable fact; in the end they are nothing but word games. This one, on the contrary, marks a definitive point in our biology.

But let us come back to that period where we left Semmelweis, that is to say about 1846. He was then far from having reached that magnificent certainty. At the time, on the contrary, everything around him was contradictory and incoherent. He searched through the reports of the Imperial Commission. Not a single one of the possible measures set forth and tested by practical application yielded any result. Not even the beginning of hope.

Semmelweis was thus thrown back upon his own resources.

It was then that he began to proceed by successive eliminations of the Past, removing the errors and lies which concealed the truth, one after another, throwing them far away as though they were the dead leaves choking the flower for which he searched. The initial fact, the point of departure once and for all in this journey of discovery was this: *The mortality rate was higher in Klein's wards than in Bartsch's.*

Everyone previously had noticed this, but no one had paid attention to it as closely. He recognised that this was the only fact gleaned in the course of a tragedy in which everything was obscure. And it was from this fact that he would build, and it was always to this starting point that he would return. There were still a hundred false trails along which he might have lost his way. He refused to follow them. At last, when, by force of persuasion and often, alas! of rudeness, he managed to convince those who were willing, or pretended to be willing, to help him with his efforts from this starting point, solutions began to pour forth. All around him, they vied with each other in ingenuity, cleverness and pride. "If there are fewer deaths in Bartsch's," maintained some of those clever fellows, fearing to be outdone, "that's because in his clinic the work is exclusively in the hands of apprentice midwives, while in Klein's students undertake the same task with the expectant mothers without any gentleness and through their roughness bring about a fatal inflammation!" For in those days it was firmly believed that inflammation was the aetiology of puerperal fever.

Hurrah! The world was saved!

Semmelweis at once seized the opportunity offered by his rivals to mount a practical test.

The midwives who had been on duty in Bartsch's clinic were exchanged with the medical students in Klein's.

Death followed the students, the mortality rate in the Bartsch wards became alarming, and Bartsch in desperation sent the students back where they had come from.

Semmelweis was now certain (and the rest could have been, had they so wished) that the students were playing a role of prime importance in this disaster. That counted for a lot. It was all that was needed to make him the centre of a deluge of advice. Even Klein, who was beginning to feel disturbed by the revolutionary changes his assistant wanted to effect in his cursed domain, Klein, whose obstetrical practice was surrounded by a tragic reputation throughout the whole of Austria, offered then the explanation that it was the foreign students who were responsible for the spread of puerperal fever.

In accordance with the wish of this chief physician expulsions were arranged, and the number of students was reduced from forty-two to twenty by the departure of the foreigners.

As a result of this measure the mortality rate fell for several weeks following...

How bewildering even such a slight improvement might have been to one who is passionately scrutinising the surface of the Unknown, we may well imagine. How much more arresting than it need have been might such evidence prove in the mind of the researcher, causing him to lose his way in useless deductions, and thus his research, a simple wagon, wavering and jolting, may become stuck in the mud for a long time, perhaps forever.

That was not the case with Semmelweis, who was inspired, thanks be to God!

He leaped over these insignificant obstacles, he wanted more, he wanted to see with absolute clarity, he wanted it with an excess of violence.

There were no degrees to that passion of his. From his want of social graces he was accused of intolerance, of a lack of respect in relation to Klein. This, alas, was also true!

Some found his arrogance insupportable; there were those who said that he was playing with "Christopher Columbus's egg".[4] In his eagerness for research, he cut himself off from everyday life, he ignored it, he no longer lived except for this passion, with such concentration, with such perseverance that he always returned to that single, tangible and demonstrated fact, that *"more women were dying in Klein's clinic with its students, than in Bartsch's with its midwives"*. Unceasingly he went on repeating to all who would or would not listen to him: "The cosmic, telluric, hygrometric causes that have been invoked concerning puerperal fever cannot be accepted as having any validity since more women are dying in Klein's clinic than in Bartsch's, in the hospital than at home, where, nonetheless, the cosmic and telluric conditions and all the rest are exactly the same."

One day, as though from afar, he perceived a brief but certain light

4. Columbus is supposed to have challenged a nobleman, who had disputed the importance of his discovery of America and claimed others could equally have done it, to stand an egg on its end. He failed. Columbus then did so by slightly breaking the base of the egg. Moral: it takes a genius to discover something which may then be easily repeated by everyone else. [Trans.]

in all this darkness. It did not surprise him, he recognised it. Is this not another remarkable quality, and perhaps the most precious for those who triumph over the unknown in the realm of science, that of being able to recognise the one certain and indispensable fact, no matter how brief its appearance may be, among all the other concurrent facts, without immediate or potential importance, and even to exceed their own abilities at that particular moment? This revelation was unambiguous.

"The cause I am seeking is in our own clinic and nowhere else," Semmelweis told Markusovszky on the evening of 14 July 1846.

However, an undercurrent of hostility, which he did not suspect, or because he held them in contempt, was directed towards him. A surge of unpleasantness began to surround his name. The words used to qualify his attitude no longer fully concealed all the hatred he had already incited.

It eventually spilled over into silence.

Klein no longer spoke to him, so bitter had their relations become in the course of five months. On the occasion of a meeting of professors, Klein had remarked, perhaps to mislead him, that the cause of the puerperal epidemics should be sought in the age of the buildings. To this Semmelweis immediately, and bluntly, replied that in the Boërs clinic, the oldest in Vienna, there was certainly a much lower mortality rate than in Klein's.

It would be a while before Klein responded definitively to the blow of this new insolence.

Thenceforth, he only looked for the first opportunity to dismiss his assistant. Semmelweis got wind of this; consequently all his nights, from this moment until his departure, were spent in the clinic, at the bedsides of the women patients and in particular with the dying ones, he sensing that his days in the hospital were numbered... That if the truth was there, under his very hands, his grasp was somehow not strong enough to draw it out of the silence, in which it was buried in a hundred different ways...

He saw, too, day by day the number of his enemies becoming ever greater, mocking his efforts, which he must quickly, absolutely, at any price, drive to a conclusion... or fall back lower into that passive herd in which he could never exist...

Days, nights, followed one another, horrible, the nights especially...

Markusovszky came to see him, and he confessed, "that he could no longer sleep, that the dispiriting sound of the bell tolling which preceded the priest carrying the viaticum had forever disturbed the peace of his soul. That all the horrors to which he was daily the impotent witness made life intolerable for him. That he could not endure his current situation in which everything was dark, in which the only thing that was known for sure was the number of deaths."

And everyone could hear the tolling of that bell. It too was therefore to be suspected (what after all was not suspected?) of instilling in the expectant mothers a state of nervousness which predisposed them to the ravages of puerperal fever. Temporarily, the ringing was suppressed. The priest made a detour on his way to the bedsides of the dying.

After this, still another subtle detail aroused a few new hopes. Had they not noticed that the unmarried women, the adolescent mothers, were more depressed than the others with the coming of their labour pains? There it was, announced the psychologists, an excellent reason! Another month or two passed, and then it was a cold spell (after the heat, after the diet, after the moon) which was held to be responsible.

While one ridiculous, insincere explanation followed another, Semmelweis made the observation that the women who, caught by surprise, came to time in the street and were only admitted later to the Klein clinic, even in the midst of those periods of so-called epidemic, were almost always spared.

Knowing already from his earlier experience that a curse had fallen especially upon the medical students, Semmelweis began to undertake a very close scrutiny of this group, studying more and more closely their comings and goings, all their habits and actions. At the same time he recalled, and all the better because he had for a long time lived with Rokitansky in the very midst of his dissections, those often fatal dissecting incisions these same students happened to inflict upon themselves with dirty instruments.

His ideas began to crystallise.

During the days that followed, he asked Rokitansky to give him Dr. Lautner as an assistant in order that he might carry out autopsies and the dissection of cadaveric tissues with his help, without moreover having any preconceived framework for this histological research. In short, they were to be "experiments to see" as Claude Bernard later called them.

At that moment he was so near the truth as to be on the point of tracing its outlines. He was even closer when he suggested that all the students should be made to wash their hands before going anywhere near the preganant women. They asked themselves the "why" of this measure; it seemed foreign to the scientific spirit of the age. It was an eccentric fancy. Nevertheless Semmelweis insisted that washstands be placed near the doors of the clinic and gave orders to all the medical students to clean their hands with the greatest care as a necessary preliminary to any investigation or manipulation of women in childbirth.

But, unconcerned at first, and then becoming hostile, proper procedure, which he had quite ignored, lay in wait to strike him down in full flight. It entered the next day in Klein's footsteps.

Semmelweis informed him, upon his arrival at the clinic, of the degree of cleanliness that he wished to instil in the medical students.

He also asked Klein to submit to this precaution himself. In what terms did he make this proposition...? Evidently Klein demanded an explanation of this preliminary washing which seemed to him, *a priori*, completely ridiculous.

Undoubtedly, he even found it irritating...

Semmelweis, for his part, was not yet in a position to offer any plausible answer or any respectable theory, since he was still at the stage of guesswork. Klein flatly refused.

On edge from so many long and exhausting sleepless nights, Semmelweis flew into a rage, forgetting the respect that was due, in spite of everything, to this least worthy of his masters.

Of course, this incident provided exactly the excuse Klein had been waiting for. The next day, 20 October 1846, Semmelweis was summarily dismissed.

In the two clinics, the Fever, threatened for a moment, now triumphed... it killed with impunity, as it wished, where it wished, when it wished... in Vienna... 28% in November... 40% in January... the circle expanded, all around the World. Death led the dance... surrounded by those tolling bells... In Paris at the Dubois clinic... 18%... 26% in the Schuldt clinic in Berlin... in Simpson's clinic, 22%... in Turin, thirty-two out of every hundred died following childbirth.

As indeed might well be expected, this incident provoked a great stir in medical circles, and even at Court, whence came the orders to open an enquiry into the circumstances surrounding this dismissal. Škoda's offices as chief physician at the General Hospital, required him, even while maintaining his neutrality, to sanction to some extent the dismissal of his pupil. Although unwilling to abandon Semmelweis's fate to his enemies, he was too well aware of the favour Klein enjoyed at Court to risk, in taking too inflexible a stance, losing for good his protégé at the same time as his own prestige. Furthermore, Škoda had many strings he could pull and knew how to do so, and when. He remembered, among other things, that for a while he had been the doctor ordinary to the Imperial family, and once Klein had been somewhat appeased, Škoda brought to bear all the weight of his influence at Court to regain for Semmelweis the post that he had lost.

The world of courtiers has scarcely any other reason for existing than for the cultivation of all sorts of intrigues, and the promotion of all those causes, good or bad, which are always to be found in such careerist circles. Such was the case for Semmelweis's career, as nurtured by Škoda. Only, isn't it usually the case that one can plot better only for those who are not present? Thus the impetuous Philipp was sent away for a short while. When a destination had to be chosen, it was Venice that was then fashionable. Alfred de Musset had returned, sobbing his adventures to the sympathetic echoes of Parnassus:

"Man is an apprentice, Sorrow is his master," sang his dolorous muse.

In the cultivated, romantic Europe of the day, to weep to the accents of his languishing lyre was the mark of a sensitive soul.

Not one artist who would not have given his life and more to experience those misty evenings on the Lido on a litter of superfluous regrets and rose petals...

Semmelweis, still staggering under such a brutal blow, was easily enrolled in the ranks of those sentimental pilgrims. One recalls his earlier taste for music, songs, and even for the gentle Apollo of *On the Life of Plants* which he had slightly neglected.

Markusovszky, his eternal friend and physician in the same hospital, was to accompany him at Škoda's request. Thus, one fine morning in spring, the two of them set out on this long journey.

Off to the city of gondoliers, barcarolles, and sighs! Farewell to disappointments!

The journey took six days.

They had to make a detour through Trieste, because the road over the Alps was still blocked by snow... Udine the golden... At Treviso they stopped for a day... Venice! There Semmelweis forgot his ordeals, his rebuffs.

His extraordinarily good and totally generous character allowed him to forget everything, except his heart. In Venice his heart beat with the same unrestrained rhythm as it had in Vienna, in its fervour for a new cause. He threw himself into the attractions of Venice and gave himself over to them entirely with the same enthusiasm by which he had been marked amongst the misery of the Klein clinic.

Hardly had he arrived than he wanted to see everything, to hear everything, to know everything. He bathed himself in Italy. Besides, he did not know how to do anything except passionately. His twenty-nine years were burning him up. Markusovszky, who went out walking with him, was exhausted by his tireless sight-seeing. The two of them were seen everywhere, and everywhere as well they were in raptures; in gondolas, on foot, in carriages, by day, by night. Nothing could stop him, neither the language of which he could not speak a word, nor the important and sumptuous History of Venice, of whose complex majesty he was utterly ignorant. But he could learn about it, and learn he did.

One, two, ten books were acquired in turn and their contents as quickly laid to waste by the curiosity of this impetuous dilettante. He also took notes in the museums, but lost them as soon as they were made, scattered here and there, for his heedlessness equalled his impatience. Eventually he grew bored of sitting still in gondolas too slow for his liking. He learned to handle these vessels himself, and was soon skilful enough to steer Markusovszky and the gondolier through the narrowest canals.

Never had Venice with its hundred marvels received a more hurried lover. And yet, among all those who have loved this city of mirages, has any expressed more resplendent gratitude than Semmelweis?

After two months spent in this great garden of all the precious stones, two months immersed in beauty, they returned to Vienna. Only a few hours passed before Semmelweis was hit with the news of the death of a friend. Was not such cruelty of fate just a normal occurrence in his life?

Kolletschka, the professor of anatomy, had just died the night before as the result of a skin-prick accidentally received in the course of a dissection. Kolletschka had always expressed the liveliest and warmest sympathy for Semmelweis; his death, isolating Semmelweis still further, was peculiarly saddening. Nevertheless, nothing that happened to him, joys no less than griefs, seemed to be without use in the elaboration of his great work. He had completely accepted his own life, and all those spiritual forces he encountered along the roads of his destiny found a way into his soul.

"I was still under the influence of Venice and its attractions, still thrilling to the artistic emotions I had felt during those two months I passed in the midst of those incomparable wonders when I heard about the death of poor Kolletschka. It put me in a state of extreme sensitivity, and when I learned all the details of the illness which had killed him, the notion that this disease was identical with the puerperal infection from which women in childbirth were dying took form so suddenly in my mind, with such blinding clarity, that I ceased from that moment to look elsewhere.

"Phlebitis... lymphangitis... peritonitis... pleurisy... pericarditis... meningitis... were all one and the same! This was what I had been looking for in all this time in the shadows, and nothing else."

Music and Beauty are within us, and nowhere else, in this unfeeling world which surrounds us.

Great works are those which awaken our genius, great men are those who give them a form.

In all that concerned himself he had no ambition, he did not any longer have that regard for pure truth which animates scientific researchers. We could say that he would never have undertaken the course of his research if he had not been dragged into it by a consuming pity for the physical and mental distress of his patients.

"He was, in short, a poet of goodness, who more than others made a reality of his dream."

When we call to mind these lines of Dr. Bruck about the amazing penetration Semmelweis achieved in the course of his successive discoveries, we are tempted to ask if indifference and egotism are not in fact the greatest obstacles to genius among the majority of physicians of great talent. This is a difficult thought, but in the course of the sudden turns of this tragic and marvellous adventure, it is impossible to avoid considering this hypothesis, especially during those critical moments in research, on the very threshold of discovery, when the truth partially reveals itself.

A half-truth is a pleasant form of failure, a tempting consolation...

To go beyond it, ordinary lucidity is insufficient, it is then that the researcher needs a strength which burns more brightly, a penetrating lucidity as keenly sensitive as jealousy. The most brilliant qualities of the mind are powerless unless they are supported by experience and determination. Talent alone would never claim to discover the true hypothesis, for it is in the nature of talent to be more ingenious than truthful.

We had felt, in considering the lives of other physicians, that these sublime ascents towards the realm of the great precise truths proceeded almost uniquely from an enthusiasm far more poetic than the rigour of experimental methods, which is generally given as their sole genesis.

The experimental method is no more than a technique, infinitely valuable, but depressing. It requires of the researcher an increase in fervour if he is not to be discouraged before attaining the goal he has set for himself, along that naked path he must follow in its company.

Man is a creature of feeling. There are no great creations outside the realm of emotion, and enthusiasm rapidly dries up amongst the majority of men in proportion as they wander from their dream.

Semmelweis was born out of a dream of hope that the unchanging environment of such atrocious suffering could never discourage, but on the contrary, all its adversities contributed to his triumph. He lived, with all his sensitivity, in the midst of lamentations so shrill that any dog would have fled, howling. But in this way, adapting his dream to all these promiscuities meant living in a world of discoveries, seeing into the night, perhaps forcing the world to enter his dream. Haunted by human suffering he wrote, on one of those very rare days when he was thinking of himself: "My dear Markusovszky, my good friend, my kind supporter, I must confess to you that my life was a living hell, that always the thought of death for my patients was unbearable to me, especially when it crept between the two great joys of living, that of being young, and that of giving life."

How valuable is such a confidence for a biographer! It brings to our understanding the inner poetry of a great discovery which in its absence might seem but harsh, brilliant, and unexplained.

Once back in Vienna, when the veil had been torn asunder, when the identity of the cause of the anatomist Kolletschka's death with those by puerperal fever no longer seemed in doubt to him, he went forward, now armed with precise facts, towards that which was still unknown.

Since, he thought, Kolletschka had died following a cadaveric skin-prick, it was therefore the exudations given off by the cadavers that one must blame for the phenomenon of contagion. As for the details of this contagion, he thought immediately he knew what they were.

"It is the fingers of the medical students, soiled by recent dissections, which carry the fatal cadaveric particles into the genital organs of the pregnant women, and especially up to the cervix of the uterus."

This conclusion was confirmed by all the clinical observations which had been made previously.

But, to go still further, he had at once to solve a great technical difficulty, important at least for the science of that period. He attacked this shrewdly, and luck also played its part.

These minute cadaveric particles, simple contact with which he believed sufficed entirely to provoke puerperal infection, were so imponderable that Histology could not yet stain them clearly enough to make them visible under the microscope. They could therefore be detected only by their odour.

"Deodorise the hands," he decided, "the whole problem is there." The method was doubtful; but it was successful enough to demonstrate to him that this cause of contagion was not enough to explain everything.

But to put into practice this prophylaxis, which was his idea, it was still necessary to have free access to one of the Maternity Hospitals of the City.

Since this proposed undertaking resembled too closely the one which had led to his expulsion from Klein's clinic, it was too much to hope for straightforward reinstatement to his former post, in spite of Škoda's extensive influence. Another door must be opened for him.

Won over by Škoda's insistence, Bartsch, chief physician of the second clinic, was persuaded to accept his protégé with the title of supplementary assistant, although at that time he really had no need of any additions to his staff.

Hardly had Semmelweis entered upon his new duties than, upon his request, the medical students, ordinarily assigned to Klein's clinic, moved to Bartsch's clinic in exchange for the midwives.

The fact so many times observed was faithfully repeated right away.

During the month of May 1847, the puerperal mortality rate rose in Bartsch's clinic to 27%, an increase of 18% on that of the preceding month. The decisive test was then undertaken. Pursuing his technical idea of deodorisation, Semmelweis decided upon a calcium chloride solution with which every medical student who had practised dissection that day or the night before was compelled to wash his hands, thoroughly, before undertaking any sort of examination of pregnant women. In the month following the application of this measure the mortality rate fell to 12%.

The result was very clear, but this was not yet the definitive triumph Semmelweis wanted. Until that moment his mind was set on the cadaveric cause of puerperal infection. This cause seemed to him henceforth to be proven, real, but fragmentary.

He avoided, dreaded, the "half-truth", he wanted the whole truth. One might almost say that during those few weeks death was seeking to trick him, was toying with him. But in the end he was the victor.

He was going to touch the microbes without seeing them.

How to destroy them, this problem still remained. He must do better. Here are the facts: in the month of June, a woman was admitted to Bartsch's clinic who was thought to be pregnant, according to poorly verified symptoms, Semmelweis in his turn examined her and discovered that she had a cancer in the uterine cervix, and then, without remembering to wash his hands, he undertook the task of delivering, successively, five women who were in the dilatation period.

In the following weeks, these five women died of typical puerperal infection.

The final veil dropped. There was light at last. "The hands, by their simple contact, may be infectious," he wrote... From that moment, each student, whether he had been practising dissection or not during the preceding days, was made to submit to careful disinfection of the hands using a solution of calcium chloride.

The result was immediate, it was magnificent. In the following month, the puerperal mortality rate became almost zero, it sank, for the first time, to the figure of the best contemporary Maternity Hospitals in the world: 0.23%![5]

5. According to the judicious remark of Professor Brindeau, these figures refer to the period of Semmelweis and not to our own, in which puerperal infection comprises the fewest cases, without taking their gravity into account. [Author's note]

> If it were discovered that the truths of
> geometry might annoy men, they would have
> been declared false a long time ago.
>
> JOHN STUART MILL

However much this philosopher appears to exaggerate, he actually understates the truth, and here is the proof. Would not the most elementary reasoning have shown that humanity, guided by its far-sighted thinkers, could have been forever rid of all death-dealing infections, and not least of puerperal fever, since that month of June 1848? Without a doubt.

But decidedly, Reason is but a tiny power in this world of ours, for it required no less than forty years for the best minds to admit, and at last to act upon, Semmelweis's discovery.

Obstetrics and Surgery spurned with an almost unanimous outburst, and with hatred, this great step forward they had been invited to take.

They preferred, out of a bizarre touchiness, to remain in their swamps of purulent stupidity, and continue their game of gambling with death.

And, moreover, it would not be through Semmelweis that this great and urgent service would triumph (precious, at least, if one may take at face value the cares men seem to take to avoid suffering and to live life pleasantly).

It is even reasonable to maintain that if Pasteur had not appeared to destroy the cult of "sufficient theories", in medical matters, if he had not fought them with realities too minute to be refuted by simple lies, no real progress would ever have been made, whether in surgery or obstetrics, in spite of the efforts of a few isolated men of great talent like Michaelis and Tarnier.

There is nothing but war in the hearts of men.

In the Vienna General Hospital, where all the tests could so easily have been made, Semmelweis's discovery was not received with the acclaim one might suppose. On the contrary.

As strange as that may seem, Klein succeeded from the very first in uniting, within the Faculty even, a large number of resolute opponents to this new method: the greater part of his colleagues, in fact. Five physicians only were of equal stature to Semmelweis: Rokitansky, Hebra, Heller, Helm, and Škoda. For that reason they were loathed. But the greatest deception practised upon this courageous group must be that contained in the various replies from foreign doctors, whom they had been set on contacting individually. "We could not doubt," wrote Heller, "that, far from local jealousies and malice, we were going to receive the complete approval of those who would not fail to find Semmelweis's experiments completely conclusive."

Alas! What should one think of that Tilanus, of Amsterdam, who did not even take the trouble to reply to Semmelweis's letter, as was the case too with Schmidt in Berlin?

Sadder still! Simpson, in Edinburgh, whose career otherwise gave ample proof of his talent, understood nothing of the revolution in obstetrics announced to him by Hebra. He evaded the issue in a few polite words, empty of meaning. Then it was that Heller, sensing a hypocritical lack of understanding, and wishing to bring the problem to a head at any price, sent to England a young Viennese doctor who was a friend of his, named Routh. His mission was to deliver a lecture before the Medical Society of London, explaining in detail the results obtained by Semmelweis in the Maternity Hospital in Vienna.

As it happened, they listened to him, even applauded him, but, in that hall filled with physicians, not one was convinced for all that. No progress crowned this attempt. Inertia triumphed in England as elsewhere. And all those we have spoken of thus far remained content, for the most part, to disdain the truth that was offered to them; others among them were much more energetic in their stupidity, even militant.

Scanzoni first of all, then Seyfert in Prague, after five and a half months of experiments in their respective clinics, publicly declared that the results reported by Semmelweis did not in any way conform with what they themselves had observed. This damning report clearly gave great pleasure to Klein's partisans, who on the strength of it claimed that the statistics published by Semmelweis in 1846 were erroneous, if not falsified. All the unleashed jealousies and vanities were given free play. The hospital staff, then the medical students, declared themselves tired "of these unhealthy washings" in calcium chloride, to which they decided henceforth it was useless to submit. In the meantime, Kivich, of Rottenau, the most celebrated obstetrician in Germany, arrived in Vienna, wishing, so he declared, to obtain first-hand information of these famous results. He even came back twice to carry on his investigations.

No more than the rest could he discover anything. He even went so far as to write as much, and took pride in it...

"When the History of human errors comes to be written," Hebra was later to declare, "it will be difficult to find examples that match this, while people will be amazed that men so competent, so specialised, could in their own chosen field remain so blind and so stupid."

But these great officials were not merely blind, unfortunately.

They were at one and the same time voluble and mendacious, and above all stupid and spiteful.

Spiteful towards Semmelweis, whose health was shattered by these incredible ordeals. From that moment, it was no longer possible for him to set foot in the hospital without being showered with abuse "no less from the patients than from the medical students and the nurses." Never has human conscience clothed itself more thoroughly with shame, nor sunk lower, than in its hatred for Semmelweis during those months in 1849.

Of course, this state of affairs could not endure in a university town;

at that moment, the scandal, extraordinary as its origins were, achieved such circulation that for a second time the Minister found himself obliged to dismiss Semmelweis, on 20 March 1849.

The very next day, defending his cause in another arena, Škoda sent to the Academy of Sciences a letter detailing the absolutely conclusive results wholly supporting Semmelweis's theory, which he had just obtained by "the experimental puerperal infection of a certain number of animals."

Then Hebra, the same evening, declared before the Medical Society of Vienna, "that Semmelweis's discovery presents so great an interest for the future of surgery and obstetrics that he asks for the immediate naming of a Commission to examine with complete impartiality the results he has obtained."

This time, angry passions knew no limits: booing broke out, and there were even fist-fights in the precincts of that dignified body.

The Minister then forbade the forming of the Commission, and at the same time ordered Semmelweis to leave Vienna as soon as possible.

All this was said, and written.

$\mathbf{P}$ursued, fleeing Austria, he was to find his own City in a state of electoral turmoil. In every quarter political groups were being organised, with yelling, and street fights; the gunfire from the Faubourg Saint-Antoine echoed along the Danube. Violence followed threats.

Revolution was marching on Budapest.

Metternich had grown old, a nation may rejuvenate itself, a man may not.

Young Hungary surprised him. In twenty years the rule he had fastened upon her had become worm-eaten.

The terrible iron brace of yesterday was today no more than an old rag worn full of holes by an army of needy bureaucrats. His absolutism provoked hilarity, an antiquated method, it was at once too heavy and too light. An idiotic cover placed over a boiling cauldron.

It came to a head on 2 December 1848.

Semmelweis made no attempt to isolate himself. Like everyone else, he was captivated by events. His friends dragged him in, patriots demanded his enthusiasm, the one thing in the world in which he was richest and most generous. He followed them; soon, he was leading them. Puerperal fever, Škoda, Klein, no one had time for any of that, least of all himself. The people were in the streets, at meetings, filled with hatred for Austria. Barricades went up in Buda. There was bloodshed, but much less than in France; anarchy here was too easy. They preferred to celebrate more rapidly gained political victories.

Those won at too great a price are sad and give pleasure to no one. Liberty is amusing on that condition alone. Then it becomes fun.

"No more serfdom!", "Freedom of the press!", "The right to assemble!", such were the watchwords. Vienna granted everything that was asked and more besides...

Vienna was afraid. Budapest was overjoyed, an innocent, dancing joy. There was dancing everywhere. All the political meetings, anti-Austrian, Liberal, ended with a ball. Semmelweis joined in. At these balls, he showed himself to be high-spirited, brilliant, in spirit and in body: *"Ein flotter Tänzer"*,[6] as Dr. Bruck said later.

And besides, he loathed the Austrians so much it was a pleasure to hear him curse them!

This energy made him a great success in society and carried him still further from medicine, to such a point that his discovery seemed no

6. "A lively dancer". [Trans.]

longer to concern him, he hardly worked at all. In the space of a few months, he had squandered the little inheritance he had received from his parents; that was no hard task: two thousand crowns.

This society he was led into frequenting, composed for the most part of politicians and artists, was ignorant of his real worth. They thought him instead a cultivated physician with fanciful ideas, a little dangerous in his originality, but very entertaining.

Society and dancing set him on his way towards the feminine. He was wasting what little time was left to him.

Finally, he was tempted by sport; at thirty, he took his first riding lesson and soon after he might be seen on horseback every morning, in the best society of Budapest. That was not all: he learned to swim in the middle of winter; at the hour of his plunge, a circle of people gathered about him. Since Venice, he had never enjoyed such amusing diversions.

Of course, that robust constitution of his permitted all these fits of frenzy; it was not so with his financial resources. Soon he would have to think about earning a living. However, the friends he had acquired during this political flurry would be of enormous help, it must be admitted, in building up his practice.

He was succeeding so well in this respect and almost without adversity, he had already acquired a certain renown, when a slight but ridiculous incident caused him the greatest harm.

On the recommendation of one of his friends, he was called one day to the bedside of Countess Gradinish, one of the greatest names in Hungary.

The case was not simple, the patient was well known, thus creating a perilous set of circumstances for the reputation of a doctor.

Several of his colleagues, previously consulted, had offered contradictory diagnoses.

The family, as we may imagine, was acutely alarmed. The diagnosis to which Semmelweis inclined after a first examination of the patient was one of the bleakest. In his opinion, it was cancer of the uterine cervix, he declared himself convinced, there was no question.

The family, gathered to hear this verdict, went away completely crushed. Count Gradinish, escorting Semmelweis to the door, earnestly sought his opinion a last time, but he was unable to offer any hope.

They had resigned themselves to the worst when, late that night, the street door was shaken by violent pounding. When it was opened, a man rushed into the hall, thrust the servant aside, clambered up the stairs and bounded into the bedroom where the count and countess were in bed. It was Semmelweis.

With no preliminaries he thrust his hand under the covers and undertook once more the examination he had already made that morning, but which he had since decided was inconclusive. A moment later, he stood up triumphant: "I congratulate you, Madame Countess," he cried, "for I have been mistaken. It isn't a cancer but a simple tumour."

Accounts of this outburst immediately began to spread in society and cost him the the majority of his best clientele.

However, we must agree that he would have lost them in any case, for war was declared during the months that followed. Buda was taken almost at once, and pillaged by an army of Croats. Famine took hold. It was a simple task for the Austrians to drive out the famished Croats, and they soon joined forces with the Russians in order to crush Hungary. The latter paid, as it were, the price of this chaos, which began shortly after the retreat of Metternich and ended with the battle of Villajos. After that great defeat, anarchy became crystallised in a new social order and in the form of a greedy and punctilious military dictatorship. Under it and by it, Hungary was regularly stripped and completely despoiled. For individuals this meant misery; for the spirit it was a night which descended from 1848 until 1867.

A night of almost complete darkness, since the majority of intellectuals were banished, especially physicians.

Balassa, provost of the University of Budapest, was thrown into prison, and nearly all the professors went into exile. Even scientific journals were forbidden. Dr. Bujatz, editor of the *Medical Gazette*, was compelled to flee to Switzerland. Only one society of physicians was permitted to meet in the whole of Hungary, once monthly, in Pest, under the official surveillance of a police superintendent.

Never had tyranny been more pervasive, more odious. They began to miss Metternich.

"We can no longer see each other, no one can keep up to date with the similar work of their peers, no experiments get duplicated, we are living in the shadows." Such was the plaint of Professor Kotanyi during the course of these terrible years. In this moral and physical poverty, none the less, men had to go on living somehow, and it was living which every moment became a painful problem for the doctors of the day. They were almost never paid. What with? Ordinary taxes were followed by emergency taxes, without counting fines and penalties. With the little that was left over, people had to eat, if only once a day. Then...

The Hungarians' joy had been of as short a duration as Semmelweis's burst of dissipation, and as the happiness he felt at living an active life, a self-seeking life as compelling for him as for other people, but with a higher and more tragic destiny which seemed always to have kept him at a distance.

In 1849 he earned a meagre living through the practice of medicine. He stayed in a room in the Landergasse, in a narrow alley. He was forced to sell the larger part of his furniture to survive. Things could hardly have gone much worse when he fell victim as well to two successive accidents, which did, this time floor him.

Within the space of a few days, he first broke his arm, and then his left leg, on one of those impossibly narrow, winding staircases which were typical of this part of town.

Because of these two fractures he was confined to his bed, quite unable then to protect himself from hunger or cold. Had it not been for the devotion of his few friends who made sacrifices so that he could eat, he doubtless would have died in misery as did so many other intellectuals in the course of that winter of 1849.

Buffetted by misfortunes, in loneliness and duress, the flame which Semmelweis carried was covered by ashes and almost went out.

His past no longer spoke to him.

It was a past too filled with enthusiasm for his worn-out heart. His strength was no longer up to the task of holding that torch aloft. He was starving.

For as long as he endured this distressing situation he lived a somnolent life, his dream grown feeble, and for one such as him who must dream in order to live, this was almost a non-existence. He lost interest in everything, he no longer wrote. His masters in Vienna became concerned as to what had happened to him. Maybe they should consider bringing him back? The hatred of Klein and the others excluded him more than ever from Faculties in Austria. One day, in Vienna, the most alarming rumours were circulated about his situation. Markusovszky, after countless representations and by making use of powerful influences, was permitted to make a trip to Budapest, then off limits. As soon as he arrived, he set out in search of Semmelweis. He had not seen him for seven years.

At first he could not find him and not until late that night did the two friends meet at last.

"At last! I have found our best friend, alive," Markusovszky wrote in a letter to Škoda, "but he has aged so much that I hardly would have recognised him had not his voice led me better than his appearance in the shadows of his room. His features are marked with deep melancholy, for good, I fear. He spoke of you and of Professor Rokitansky in the most affectionate terms, and he asked a hundred questions about your life and your health. He said nothing about his material worries, which were all too evident, alas! Armed with your letters of recommendation, I called on Professor Birley, director of the St. Rochus Maternity Hospital; he gave me a strong assurance that he would consider Semmelweis for the first vacancy as assistant in his clinic. That would be some sort of justice! He remains silent about his work in Vienna.

"Soon this will be seven years of silence...

"I shall relate the rest to you personally."

And Markusovszky left for Vienna a few days later.

In the months that followed, Semmelweis did nothing to bestir himself, he did not even go to see Birley, who had meanwhile, in a friendly letter, invited him to call.

Thus his days dragged along, and shunning all effort he no longer had any expectations, when a chance event directed him back towards his destiny.

"Aren't you the Dr. Semmelweis, formerly assistant to Professor Klein?" a certain visitor asked one morning.

"..."

"If so, I have a message for you. A painful message, but one which favours the cause you used to support. Here are the facts: Professor Michaelis, of Kiel, committed suicide recently under very strange circumstances; I was his student and I knew all his thoughts, especially the one which obsessed him and drove him to suicide. He had recently attended a cousin of his in her lying-in, but a few days later she succumbed to puerperal infection.

"So overwhelming was Michaelis's grief, so frightful his despair, that he made an immediate and very detailed investigation into his own responsibility in this tragic case. He could not defer the conclusion that he himself was entirely responsible, because, in the days before, he had as it happened been treating a fair number of women stricken with puerperal fever without afterwards taking any of the precautions you had indicated and with which he had been long familiar.

"The obsession which overwhelmed him became one day so piercing, so unbearable, that he threw himself in front of a train..."

At this moment, Semmelweis emerged from his torpor as though roused by the singing of this arrow which had just cut through his silence...

There and then he went to call upon Birley to ask if he might resume his work in obstetrics.

Birley was a courageous man, impressed with Semmelweis, but he had no desire to see what had occurred in the Maternity Hospital in Vienna repeated in his own wards. He received Semmelweis cordially, but upon certain conditions.

"You have been recommended to me," he said, "by Professor Škoda and that is enough to guarantee for you my entire goodwill. Nevertheless I am not able, in the present state of our Maternity Hospital, to offer you work except during the two vacation months, July and August. In addition, I must ask you to say nothing to my medical students about this washing their hands in calcium chloride, that would do us the greatest damage...

"I have, it should be added, given deep thought to those frightful mortality rates that you once observed in Klein's clinic and I shall, myself, tell you what I believe is the reason. Klein did not prescribe regular purges for his lying-in patients. Now here..."

Docile for a change, Semmelweis managed for once to keep his mouth shut; he thus entered upon his brief duties as a substitute and there began the editing of his supreme work: *The Aetiology of Puerperal Fever.*

T his distilling of the observations he had made at the Maternity Hospital in Vienna took him more than four years. He wrote slowly, painfully, in secret, so as not to lose his humble appointment nor agitate the timorous Birley, by whom he knew he was being watched. However, as no other echo of his discovery percolated through from abroad, he wrote a second time, after a silence of six years, to Seyfert, to the great Virchow, to many others, but no one replied.

"Of all the obstetricians I know," he then wrote, "that poor Michaelis is decidedly the first and the only one of whom it might be said that he had too great a professional conscience." It was true; and that truth became monstrous when, after he had sent a report containing a summary of his findings to the Paris Academy of Medicine, that body, through the intermediary of a Commission presided over by Orfila, did not deign to answer him. We do not know why its deliberations were kept secret.

During this time, the material and moral conditions in his homeland would grow a little better. So much so that for the first time, in the year

1855, he earned a little amount to satisfy his needs: 400 florins.

Time passed.

In 1856 Birley died.

Semmelweis succeeded him as director of the St. Rochus Hospital.

He seemed to be free now to undertake his initiatives in obstetrical practice.

We must note that it had been thought that he had been silenced for good by fear, or by his mistake! It was a real surprise to discover that he was more aggressive even than he had been in Vienna. Not all his intiatives turned out well, especially his opening gesture! For example: his "Open Letter to all Professors of Obstetrics", in which he undertook to break a silence that had lasted ten years.

"I would have preferred that my discovery might have been found to be a part of the realm of physics, for one may explain light just as one likes, but that does not prevent it from shining, it is independent of physicists. My discovery, alas! depends upon obstetricians! That changes everything...

"Assassins! that is what I call all those who protest against the rules which I prescribed to combat puerperal fever.

"Against them I stand as a resolute opponent, as one should stand against those who have committed a crime! For myself, I cannot regard them as anything other than assassins. And all those whose hearts are in the right place will think as I do! It is not the lying-in clinics that should be closed to put a stop to the deplorable disasters of which they are the scene, but rather it is the obstetricians who should be made to quit them, for it is they themselves who behave like real epidemics," and so on.

If these truths seemed too urgent, it was nevertheless childish to express them in this insufferable manner. The hatred aroused by this pamphlet became only the amplified echo of that whose violence he had experienced ten years before in Vienna.

In that oppressed city, plunged into an atmosphere of dismay in which it seemed that the pettymindedness especially of medical practice must be naturally silenced, this was not the case. In that very hospital where Semmelweis had become physician-in-chief, so much meanness was uncovered, so much professional foul-play, that his prescriptions against puerperal fever were never willingly observed. It even seems that infection might have been deliberately spread among the obstetrical patients for the ghastly satisfaction of proving him wrong. This is not mere supposition, since figures show that under the direction of old Birley only 2% of the obstetrical patients in the St. Rochus Maternity Hospital died from puerperal fever, while under Semmelweis this figure rose to 4% in 1857, then 7% in 1858, and finally to 12% in the year 1859.

There were unimaginable horrors, for example, that letter from a municipal councillor of Buda to Professor Semmelweis in which "the

City refuses absolutely to pay for the hundred pairs of sheets ordered by him on account of his hospital." "A useless purchase," declared the councillor, "since several deliveries can very well be performed in succession using the same sheets."

A complete hostility, as not long since in Vienna, established itself from that point onwards in opposition to all his decisions. Only one single friend remained, following the desertion of all those whose sympathies he had been counting on. That friend, alas! exercised no official influence, but he was young, active and generous. This was Dr. Arneth.

He was fired up by Semmelweis's cause, and wanted to go as far as Paris to defend it and bring about its triumph.

From there, it seemed to him, all ideas acknowledged as valuable could easily make their way into the world.

In line with his delusion, he saw France as a Republic of minds as well as laws.

Had not its two Revolutions demonstrated this?

Together, the two men dreamed of official experiments upon which the great masters of French science would pronounce a definitive verdict.

With endless trouble they succeeded in collecting money enough for that daring journey. A passport was still more difficult to obtain. At last, carrying with him the manuscript of *The Aetiology*, Arneth set out on 13 March 1858.[7]

If one could write the hidden history of true human events, what a precarious moment, what a perilous moment that journey would constitute!

But it is no less true that the span and the sorrows of men count for little, in the long run, compared to the passions, the absurd frenzies which make History dance to the score of Time.

No sign revealed to those who met him on his way to Paris that this poor, lonely traveller, the son of a second-rate nation, carried in his luggage a sheaf of pages more precious than all the secret books of all the Indies, that he was the bearer of a wonderful truth, the simple reading of which might every year save the lives of thousands of human beings, and spare them infinite suffering.

To his fellow companions in the stage-coach, he was a poor traveller, nothing more; were he to speak of what he knew, he would bore everyone; if he insisted too much, might he have been killed? Goodness is but a small mystical current among all the others and its indiscretion is tolerated with reluctance.

In contrast, look at War as it marches by: nothing is too gilded, too clamorous, too immodest for it.

The general's glory is the sort which can be understood at once, it

---

7. 18 March according to certain authorities. [Author's note]

is dazzling, it is huge, it is expensive.

A great benefactor will always seem, whatever is said or whatever is done, a bit banal, his fineness will appear a little common, like that of the sun or water. Collective intelligence is a superhuman task.

In Paris, where Arneth stayed for several weeks, the Academy of Medicine was devoting a certain number of conferences, as it happens, between 23 February and 6 July 1858, to the study of problems concerning puerperal fever.

Arneth did not fail to attend these meetings. His hopes were dashed, however, when he understood how completely they wanted not to know the truth in that arena, and especially when he had heard the most celebrated obstetrician of his time, Dubois, sum up the opinion of that learned gathering in the course of a most regrettable speech: "This theory of Semmelweis which, it may perhaps be remembered, provoked such violent polemics in obstetrical circles, no less in Austria than in other countries, seems today to be completely abandoned, even in the school in which it was once professed.

"It may be that it did contain a few good principles, but its scrupulous application presented such difficulties that it was necessary, in Paris for instance, to place the hospital staff in quarantine for a large part of the year, and that, moreover, for an altogether problematical result."

What to do in the face of such a gainsayer? Arneth could not imagine confronting him. He tried to obtain permission for some experiments to be undertaken in Parisian hospitals on the model of those which had been carried out in Vienna by Semmelweis formerly, but after only a short time he had to give up, meeting only hostility in some quarters, timidity in others, and everywhere a blind submission to the verdict of Dubois, the uncontested and reigning master of obstetrics in France.

Returning to Budapest, the discouraged Arneth could not succeed in convincing Semmelweis of what he had seen and heard, and especially of the futility of all future effort.

Arneth remained reasonable, Semmelweis could be so no longer.

To calculate, to foresee, to wait, seemed especially impossible tyrannies to his bewildered mind.

Doubtless he had already overstepped the wise boundaries set up by our common sense, that great tradition of our minds which says that we are all little children, sweetly linked by custom to the chain of Reason which ties together, whether one wishes it or not, the most inspired and the most ignorant amongst us, from the first to the last day of our communal life. By breaking a link in this heavy chain Semmelweis freed himself from it... and hurled himself into incoherence. He had lost his lucidity, that power of all powers, that concentration of all our hopes upon one specific point in the Universe. Without this, how to choose in this fleeting life a form of the world that suits us? How not to lose one's path? If man has ennobled himself amongst the animals, has it not been because he has succeeded in discovering a greater number of facets in the Universe?

He is the most ingenious courtier of nature and his shifting and fluid happiness, inclining from life towards death, is his insatiable reward.

How perilous is this sensibility! To what ceaseless labour is he not condemned to maintain the balance of this fragile marvel!

Hardly indeed except in his deepest slumber can his spirit find rest. Absolute inertia is for the brutes, our human structure forbids it to us. Slaves to Thought, that's it, that's what we all are. Simply opening one's eyes, is that not immediately balancing the world on the top of one's head? To drink, to talk, to be amused, perhaps to dream, doesn't that mean making an unceasing choice, between all the varying aspects of the world, those that are human and traditional, and then tirelessly dismissing the others, until fatigue inevitably catches up with us at the end of every day?

Shame upon him who knows not how to choose the aspect suited to the destiny of our species! He is stupid, he is mad.

As for our imagination, and the originality with which our pride flatters itself, their limits, alas! too are fixed and weighed down by discipline! No imagination is permitted except that which yet rests upon the illusory granite of good sense. Stray too far from this convention and neither reason nor other minds will understand you. Semmelweis was wasting his energy when he transformed all his courses into long abusive denunciations of all professors of obstetrics.

He ended up making himself both intolerable and ineffective by going round and posting on walls in the town manifestos from which we can quote these words: "Fathers of families, do you know what it means to call to the bedside of your wife in labour a doctor or a midwife? It means you are voluntarily making her run the risk of losing her life, so easily avoidable by these measures...", etc.

Without a doubt he would, from that moment, have been relieved of his duties if his progressive exhaustion had not made such harshness unnecessary. Soon, in fact, the words he uttered did not convey what he wanted them to and were most often meaningless. His body became bent in a new and shuddering gait; he seemed in the eyes of everyone to be always hesitating on the threshold of an unknown territory...

They caught him digging into the walls of his bedroom, in search, he explained, of the great secrets buried there by a priest of his acquaintance. In the course of a few months melancholy had cut deeply into his features, and his gaze, bereft of the support of substance, seemed to lose itself behind whoever he was talking to.

He swiftly became the puppet of all his faculties, once so powerful, but now let slip into absurdity.

Laughter possessed him one moment, then vindictiveness, then kindness, in turn, completely, and in no logical sequence, each of his feelings acting on their own account, seeming desirous only of draining the powers of the unfortunate man even more thoroughly than the preceding frenzy. A personality is drawn and quartered every bit as cruelly as a body when madness turns the wheel of its torture.

Do not heed those poets who go about lamenting the rigours and subjection of thought or who curse the material chains which hold down, so they claim, their marvellous flight towards the heaven of pure spirit! Happy their lack of insight! Pretentious ingrates in truth, who can only imagine one pretty little corner of that absolute liberty they feign to desire so much! Suppose they suspected, this reckless band, that hell begins at the doorway of our monumental Rationality they despise, and against which, in their senseless revolt, they sometimes go so far as to smash their lyres! If they only knew! With what overwhelming gratitude would they not sing of the sweet limitation of our minds, that happy prison of the senses which protects us with an infinite intelligence and of which our subtlest lucidity gives but a mere glimpse. Semmelweis had escaped from the warm refuge of Reason, in which has been entrenched forever that enormous yet fragile power of our species in a hostile universe. Now he wandered with the mad, into the absolute, into those glacial solitudes where our passions no longer awaken echoes, where our terror-stricken human heart, beating fit to burst on the road to the Void, is no more than a stupid and disorientated little animal.

Penetrating into this pitiless and shifting maze of dementia, Michaelis now appeared to him, bleeding and heavy with reproaches; Škoda, enormous, coarse; Klein, furious, accusatory, livid with all the hatred of an infernal world; Seyfert, and then Scanzoni...

Things, people, more things, the heavy currents of unnamable terrors, vague forms together dragged him into the circumstances of his past, parallel, intersecting, menacing, dissolving...

All about him, the real, the banal intensified the absurd by means of an evil trick of his unlimited mind. The tables, the lamp, his three chairs, the window, all the most neutral and familiar objects of his everyday life were now surrounded by a mysterious aura, by a hostile light. Nothing to hold on to henceforth in this grotesque flux in which contours, causes and effects all liquefied. To that room now removed by his madness outside of space and time, fantastic visitors kept on returning.

With each of these he took up once more the controversy of other days; he argued at length, logically sometimes and often well past their departure. But, almost always, these hallucinations ended in violence. There were too many of these mocking, lying shadows around his bed, too many for him to see all of them, and to pick out their faces. But could he not hear them plotting behind his back, these deceitful enemies?

And his fury choked when they fled before him, oftentimes he chased after them down the staircase and even pursued them into the street.

This phase of his mental distress lasted until April 1865. At that moment, the hallucinations which had terrorised him suddenly stopped. But this was only a false improvement in his condition, barely a respite, during which, however, the surveillance he had been placed under was relaxed. He was even allowed to take a few walks in the town. He would go off through the warm streets, almost always without a hat. Everyone knew of his misfortune and each one stood aside to make way for him... It was during this lull that the Faculty decided to make a replacement for him. A delegation of his colleagues, with a great deal of circumspection, persuaded him to accept this academic measure. It was understood, in addition, that he would retain the title of "unattached" Professor. He seemed to accept this decision willingly, but later that afternoon he was seized by a crisis of dementia more intense than any before.

At two o'clock he was seen rushing through the streets, pursued by the mob of his imaginary enemies. Howling, his clothes in disarray, he arrived at the anatomy theatre of the Medical Faculty. In the centre of the room a corpse lay stretched out on the marble ready for a demonstration. Semmelweis, seizing a scalpel, pushed through the circle of medical students and overturned several chairs, he approached the slab, cut through the skin of the corpse and deep into the putrid tissues before anyone could restrain him, randomly slicing off shreds of muscle and hurling them far and wide. These actions were accompanied by exclamations and unrepeatable phrases...

The medical students recognised him, but his manner was so threatening that none dared interrupt him... He no longer knew... Now he took up the scalpel again and with his fingers and the blade rummaged about in a cavity in the corpse oozing with liquefaction. With a movement more convulsive than before, he cut himself deeply. His wound bled. He cried out. He made threats. He was disarmed. A crowd gathered around. But it was too late...

As Kolletschka not long since, he had just infected himself fatally.

The Night of the World is illuminated by divine lights.

ROMAIN ROLLAND

Škoda, notified of this culminating misfortune, set out at once for Budapest. But hardly had he arrived than he returned again, taking Semmelweis with him. What suffering there was in the course of that long journey by stage-coach! What an ordeal for the older man and the poor, wounded Semmelweis, delirious, and dangerous perhaps! What hopes still fluttered before them to risk so desperate a venture? Did Škoda envisage for a while a surgical intervention?... But he did not dwell on it, for upon reaching Vienna, on the morning of 22 June 1865, Semmelweis was immediately placed in an insane asylum.

His room, which may still be visited today, was located at the end of a long corridor, in the left wing of the building. He died there, on 16 August 1865, in the forty-seventh year of his life, following a death-agony which lasted three weeks. His old Master walked with him these last, most faltering steps of his life. For Škoda this madhouse was sadly familiar. A few years before, he had been one of the physicians there, having been banished from the General Hospital by disciplinary measures.

This had been at the very beginning of his career, in 1826, at the time when Klein (the same one, alas!), whose assistant he too had been, had packed him off to this insane asylum, on the pretext that he "tired out patients by sounding them too frequently."

In the course of these last three weeks, he doubtless pondered on the strange harmony of these troubling coincidences. Perhaps also his memory held the secret that was too painful for his heart? For like happiness, vengeance can never be complete and yet is always heavy enough to surprise one...

Twenty times night fell in that room before death carried away the one who had issued it so specific and unforgettable a challenge. In the end, it claimed only the shadow of a man, a delirious, corrupted form, whose contours were being worn away by a creeping purulence. Moreover, what victory could Death expect in this most fallen place in the whole world? Who would quarrel over these phantoms of humanity, these dissembling strangers, these grim smiles prowling along the edge of the void, on the paths of the Asylum?

Prison for instincts, Asylum for madmen, let who wants them take these howling, hurrying, whining and deranged souls.

Man ends where madness begins, the animal is a higher form and the lowest serpent can at least wriggle like its parents.

Semmelweis was even lower than all these, powerless among the mad, and more rotten than a corpse.

The progress of the infection had been so slow, so systematic, that he was not spared a single battle along the road to rest.

Lymphangitis... Peritonitis... Pleurisy... When the turn came for meningitis he began to babble a sort of endless verbal stream, an interminable reminiscence, in the course of which his broken head seemed to empty itself in long, dead phrases. It was no longer the infernal reconstitution of his life on a plane of delirium whose tormented protagonist he had been in Budapest in the first period of his madness. Fever consumed all his tragic energies. He was now only connected with the living by the formidable momentum of his past.

On the morning of 16 August, Death seized him by the throat. He suffocated.

Putrid odours flooded the room. It was finally time for him to go. But he clung on in this world as long as one can with an impossible brain and a body in tatters. He seemed to have fainted, lost in shadow, when one last revolt, very near the end, brought him up towards the light and the pain. Suddenly he raised himself up on his bed. They had to force him down again. "No! No!..." he cried out several times. It seems that in the depths of this being there could be no indulgence for the common fate, for Death, and nothing was possible for him but an enormous faith in life. He was heard again to call "Škoda!... Škoda!...", whom he didn't recognise. He entered into peace at seven o'clock that evening.

Conclusion

So here is the unhappy story of I.P. SEMMELWEIS, born in Budapest in 1818 and dying in Vienna in 1865.

He was a very great soul and a great genius in medicine. He remains, beyond any doubt, the clinical precursor of antisepsis, for the methods advocated by him, to prevent puerperal fever, are still and always will be relevant. His work is eternal. Nevertheless, it was, during his time, completely unrecognised.

We have tried to throw into relief some of the reasons which seem to us to explain a little of the extraordinary hostility of which he was the victim. But all cannot be explained by facts, words, ideas. There is, in addition, everything that one does not know, and everything one never will know.

Pasteur, with a more powerful light, was to make plain, fifty years later, the truth about microbes, in a complete and irrefutable manner.

As for SEMMELWEIS, it seems that his discovery exceeded the powers of his own genius. That, perhaps, was the deepest cause of all his misfortunes.

Louis-Ferdinand Céline

Read by: Brindeau,
President of the Thesis Jury

Read by: Roger,
Dean of the Academy

Read by, and permission granted for printing: Appell,
Rector of the Academy of Paris

TO PROFESSOR BRINDEAU
PROFESSOR OF OBSTETRICS IN THE FACULTY OF MEDICINE IN PARIS
OFFICER OF THE LÉGION D'HONNEUR
PRESIDENT FOR THIS THESIS

To whom we express our most sincere gratitude for the moral support he has given us, for his long-suffering textual criticism, without which we would not have been able to undertake this work.

We entreat him again to accept our gratitude for his scientific and literary advice , so valuable and so enlightened, which allowed us to find our way through such a saddening subject beset by names and figures.

TO THE MEMBERS OF THE JURY FOR THIS THESIS:

TO PROFESSOR FOLLET
OFFICER OF THE LÉGION D'HONNEUR
DIRECTOR OF THE SCHOOL OF MEDICINE IN RENNES
CORRESPONDING MEMBER OF THE ACADEMY OF MEDICINE
In witness of my fond admiration.

TO PROFESSOR GUNN
OF THE ROCKEFELLER FOUNDATION
KNIGHT OF THE LÉGION D'HONNEUR
With the expression of our deep gratitude.

TO HENRI MARÉCHAL
HEAD OF CLINIC IN THE FACULTY OF MEDICINE IN PARIS
Our thanks for his inexhaustible kindness and such valued support which he has always lavished upon us.

Bibliography

SEMMELWEIS: *Die Äetiologie, der Begriff und die Prophylaxe des Kindbettfiebers* (Hartleben, Pest-Vienna-Leipzig, 1861)
    Two Open Letters to Dr. Spaeth, 1861
    Two Open Letters to Dr. Scanzoni, 1861
    Two Open Letters to Dr. Siebold, 1861
BRUCK, D.: *Ignaz Philipp Semmelweis* (Teschen, Vienna, 1887)
HEGAR, A.: *I.P. Semmelweis* (Tubingen, Freiburg, 1882)
    Discours, 1882
SINCLAIR, W: *Semmelweis, His Life and His Doctrine* (Manchester, 1909)
BLUMBERG: *P.I. Semmelweis, Prinzipien des Asepsis* (Berlin, 1906)
GLOCKNER: *Gedenkblatt zur Enveilung* (Säch. Hebam. Zeit, Dresden, 1906)
GYÖRGY, T. Von: Several works (Budapest, 1886-1901)
Lancet (The): "Monument to Semmelweis" (London, 1892)
HOLMES, Oliver Wendell: *P.I. Semmelweis* (London, 1909)
ROSE: *Semmelweis* (New York Medical, 1904)
TENNESVARY: *Enthüllung, Semmelweis Denkmal* (Berlin, 1906)
WECKERLING: *Semmelweis oder Lister?* (Munich, 1907)
YOUNG, I.: *P.I. Semmelweis. A Biography* (New Zealand, 1909)
HERGOT: *Essai d'une histoire de l'obstétrique* (Masson, 1902)
PINARD: *Discours d'inauguration du monument de Semmelweis* (Budapest, 1906)

ATLAS PRESS

For our complete catalogue go to:
www.atlaspress.co.uk